SPANKR

A COLLECTION OF SHORT STORIES

BY MAGGIE WHITLEY

To Albert — with love. Maggie xx

Copyright © 2024 by Maggie Whitley
All rights reserved.

No part of this publication may be reproduced, distributed, or transmitted in any form or by any means, including photocopying, recording, or other electronic or mechanical methods, without the prior written permission of the publisher, except as permitted by UK copyright law. For permission requests, contact the author at
maggiewhitley5@gmail.com

The story, all names, characters, and incidents portrayed in this production are fictitious. No identification with actual persons (living or deceased), places, buildings, and products is intended or should be inferred.

Book Cover by Piers Schofield
Illustrations by Piers Schofield

ALSO BY MAGGIE WHITLEY

THE KETTLE QUARTET:

The Adventures of the Great Alfonso

The Kettles Boil

BUSHED!

The Man With the Tattooed Eyebrows

OTHER WORKS:

Cuddles and Custard

Plug

Arctic Moment

Green

Posthumously Yours

FOR GLYN

CONTENTS

SPANKR 1

FIVE PAST SOUTHAMPTON 33

DEAD AND GORN 83

SO 117

POPPADOMS 167

THREE SHETLAND PONIES 181

Hands, Knees and... 244

1
SPANKR

...

The bucolic village of Tickbourne cum Magna was, in the words of its 504 inhabitants, the perfect place to live. Most agreed that, despite its somewhat quirky name, it was a truly idyllic haven. A few had even gone so far as to say that many other '- ics' you could think of could equally apply to this delightful, characterful collection of houses and cottages situated on the north bank of the River Barf. The south bank was mostly water meadows as far as the eye could see, prone to flooding after heavy rains and the residents of Tickbourne blessed their forefathers who had the good sense to build their first settlement on the north side of the river, on the gentle but sufficiently elevated slopes above the river and its ings. The village boasted a 12th century church built from limestone mined not more than two miles away and its gravestones, built from the same material, recorded the surprising longevity of the locals. Most put the exceptional staying power of the Fleas, as the villagers were unimaginatively and rather unkindly known within the county, down to the presence of the pub, The Heron Fancier, which had long stood in the shadow of the church. But if anyone from the village wanted or needed sustenance, other than the spiritual or liquid variety, then the town of Barrowminster, some 15 miles away, was the source of all nourishment.

It was true that most of the population of Tickbourne was retired as few younger folk were drawn to a village where there was little employment and the highlight of the year, seemingly, was the Blessing of the Birch Bud, a custom dating back to the 13th century, a ceremony which heralded the arrival of spring. This was now performed manfully each year by the vicar, Mark Chapple, who lived in a small cottage next to the church with his wife, Angel. Apart from blessing twigs, clearly not a full-time occupation, the vicar's work mostly consisted of looking after the religious needs of his surprisingly constant congregation. The only other people gainfully employed in the village were the two ladies who ran the pub, Mrs Drax and Ms Hinkley, and several ageing farmers who, with their wives, lived high on the hills overlooking Tickbourne in small windswept cottages that had been passed down from generation to generation. The farmers tended small flocks of Flitwick Feather sheep, a local breed famous for their prodigious fleeces. They were also known, coincidentally, for their impressive life span but, perhaps surprisingly, their almost inedible meat. No-one could explain why these sheep could live for more than 20 years but their proximity to the pub was never cited as an explanation.

Several years back, a young interloper from London who was certainly no more than in his mid 40s, had tried to set up a pottery in the village. Lured by the idea of a rural retreat in one of the prettiest villages he had ever seen and with the peace and quiet required to let his creative juices flow, he'd set up a studio with a kiln in the shed in his small back garden and hung his shingle above the front door of his rented cottage. 'Toss Pot' it read. The Fleas could only agree. They frowned in unison, agreeing that the tone of the village was not exactly enhanced by this crass attempt at humour. Being a sensitive soul, as all artists are, the young man felt strangely unsettled in Tickbourne. There was nothing he could ever put his finger on - the villagers were polite but distant - but even after living there for over three months, he was still unnerved by the way the Fleas fell silent whenever he entered the pub. Perhaps, after all, a pastoral idyll was not for him, especially as he had to drive 30 miles every day for his copy of The Guardian and a packet of menthol cigarettes. He'd upped and left, taking his youth and artistry with him but leaving his pots behind, escaping back to the safety of the capital.

He had been the youngest person the village had seen for a long time. It was not as if the Fleas didn't want young blood - they did. Just not his sort. Most of them had had children of their own but they knew that as soon as they could, the youngsters would leave the village for the bright lights of Barrowminster and beyond, returning only when they thought they'd lived their lives to the full and had come to realise that the village was really rather a splendid place in which to retire after all. Bucolic it certainly was. And idyllic. Pacific too. But there was more to Tickbourne than met the eye and it was only when they returned that they realised things had never been quite what they'd seemed.

Angel Chapple, the vicar's wife, was a fine looking woman. In her stockinged feet she stood over 6 feet tall. Slim, with what can best be described as 'country looks' - glowing skin, bright blue eyes, a cheery smile - she was known throughout the village as Angel although her real name was Angela. There was debate amongst the villagers as to whether this was because of her vicarious connection to the church, St Pancreas, or whether it was due to her gossamer-fine naturally blonde hair which surrounded her head like a halo. Or maybe it was that she was simply goodness personified. Perhaps it was a combination of all three but whatever, nothing was too much bother for her. If she had been unfortunate enough to have lived several centuries ago, she would have been the one visiting the poor and needy, a small wicker basket on her arm containing an oddly shaped root vegetable or some curdled milk from her own emaciated cow. She would have held the hands of the destitute as they died from poverty and starvation. Or wiped the runny noses of their far too numerous bare-foot offspring. Perhaps held a grizzling baby in her arms until, mesmerised by her beatific face, it fell asleep in wonderment and awe. Now her pastoral activities were slightly more mundane but a lot easier. Her wicker basket had been replaced by a dozen or so plastic bags from Tesco as she did a weekly shop for the infirm who were unable or, possibly, disinclined to drive to Barrowminster themselves. No bus service had ever graced Tickbourne and taxis were as rare as rocking horse poo, so for those in need of shopping, Angel was it. And with no babies or children to attend to, either hers or anyone else's and no cow to milk, she could turn her attention to other things.

At least once a day Angel would walk around the village, whatever the weather. There were several reasons for this. She enjoyed the exercise. Angel loved walking and she could think of no better place to indulge her passion. In her mind, Tickbourne was perfection itself and the village had the simultaneous effect of energising and relaxing her. She always returned home refreshed and with a clear mind. Angel also appreciated the benefit, for both herself and her husband, of time spent away from each other. Angel needed to keep busy and a walk round Tickbourne did her no end of good. It was also good for her dog, Banjo, a wire-haired mutation rescued from having been abandoned at Tesco. At least, she'd decided it had been abandoned. The dog was yowling piteously when she'd first seen it in the car park, tied to a rubbish bin with a piece of twine. Having completed her philanthropic shopping, Angel saw that the dog was still there an hour and a half later. She decided to take matters into her own hands and immediately adopted the mutt. She named him there and then after the musical instrument she'd always wanted to play. Banjo was catchier than Euphonium and would attract less attention when she called him to heel. The dog enjoyed the walks too though there was no evidence to suggest the exercise cleared his mind and a daily walk kept Angel in touch with what was happening in Tickbourne. For a small village, things were afoot, if you knew where to look.

Once a month Angel visited every house, cottage and farmhouse in the village as well as the pub, to deliver the parish magazine, The Tickbourne Tattler. She'd started the newsletter shortly after she and Mark had arrived in the village some three years ago, seeing a need to update the residents with such significant information as the timings of the church services, the arrivals and departures, either temporary or permanent, of Fleas and anything which might affect the general day to day ebb and flow of small-village life. Anything which could disturb the rhythm of the village was recorded here; a change in the blackboard menu in the pub; an outbreak of Sheep Trots up on the farms; a Council proposal (unlikely ever to come to fruition since it was completely unnecessary), to install speed bumps outside the church. It was hardly heady or life-changing stuff but, for the Fleas, it informed them of what was going on in their small corner of the world whilst occasionally providing a window onto greater matters.

The Tattler was Angel's pride and joy and although she alone was responsible for its production and circulation, she invited contributions from the villagers. TT, as it was known, was read avidly, two sheets of foolscap devoured as if it contained the recipe for eternal life. But for most of the Fleas the unarguable highlight was a fairly recent addition penned by someone who went by the name of Spankr. This contribution, found on the back page, tucked away in the bottom right-hand corner, caused the most excitement. No-one knew who Spankr was but the information and advice they provided was invaluable and added a whole new dimension to life in Tickbourne.

"Morning Mrs Chapple."

"Good morning, Matthew."

Angel smiled broadly at the postman. Despite the fact that the temperature was hovering just above freezing the man was, as usual, wearing shorts. "Don't you find it a bit cold this morning?"

"Nah! Not me. I've known worse." He bent down to pat Banjo on the head.

Matthew was Tickbourne born and bred. He'd never travelled further than the county border, having no desire whatsoever to leave the confines of Swithinshire and everything it had to offer. What could possibly be out there that would tempt him to leave what he knew and loved? He knew many who'd gone and come back but for him, he could no more have left the village than he could have sprouted wings and flown to the Outer Hebrides. Educated minimally in Barrowminster, he'd left school with three 'O' levels and a certificate showing him to be capable of swimming underwater for 10 yards. These qualifications enabled him to get a job as a postman, a position he'd held for the past 40 years. He knew everyone in the village; he knew their histories, their peccadilloes and their secrets. Not that Mrs Chapple had any of the latter, he was sure of that.

"I see you keep making that same spelling mistake in the Parish magazine again." Matthew prided himself on his reading skills. After all, one of his O levels was for English. Nothing got past him.

"Really?" said Angel pleasantly.

Matthew nodded. "A typo they call it, I believe."

"Oh. And I'm usually so thorough. Do you remember what it was?"

"I do." Matthew put his postbag down and rummaged inside. He produced a folded copy of the magazine and handed it to her. "See!" He pointed to the back page where the word Spankr was highlighted in red.

Angel smiled. "That's not a typo, Matthew. That's how the author spells it. Like Beardr. That has a letter 'e' missing too."

Matthew looked puzzled. "Why would you do that?"

"I think it's some sort of trendy thing."

"But what does it mean? What is a Beardr?"

"As far as I know, it's a dating app for people with beards. Men, I mean. Although I can't think of any good reason why a woman might not have a beard. We have to accept that anything's possible these days."

"What's a dating app?" he asked.

"It's when you go online, on a computer, to find a date."

"Is that what Spankr is, then?"

Angel shook her head. "I don't think so. I think it's more to do with what you do when you've got a date."

"Like going to the pub for a drink? That sort of thing?"

Matthew had never been married and Angel was pretty sure he'd never even had a date in his life. But his questions were starting to get awkward.

"That sort of thing," she replied.

Matthew nodded. "Well that's cleared that up, then. Although I haven't the faintest idea what Spankr is going on about. Do you?"

Angel didn't reply.

"I wonder who Spankr is." He paused. "It's not you, is it?"

"Me?" Angel sounded genuinely horrified.

"Someone from the village then? Do you know who it is?"

"Sorry Matthew, as producer of the Tattler, I can't tell you. I'm bound by privacy laws. I'm sure you can understand that." It was the best she could come up with but Matthew accepted it without question.

"Righto, Mrs Chapple. Understood. Best be on my way." With that, he shouldered his postbag, gave her a mock salute and headed off down the road.

Angel had finished her delivery in the main part of the village and now only had the farms to do. It was a steep climb up the Tickbourne Downs and one which she enjoyed enormously. Every now and then as she followed the unpaved track up towards Ramsbottom Farm she would stop, turn round and breathe it all in. Angel felt as if she was not just taking in the view but absorbing it. She was exhilarated by the sweeping vista, sensing an almost physical pleasure from the village and its surroundings. As Tickbourne, protected on one side by the hills and the other by the water meadows, became smaller, her delight at how safe it all felt increased tenfold. This was home. She couldn't imagine wanting to be anywhere else. Perhaps I'm turning into the postman, she mused. I don't want to leave here. Ever. She took a deep breath and plodded on.

As she reached the farm gate she put Banjo on the leash. The farmyard was full of sheep and in the middle of them stood their shepherd.

"Hello Eli. Got your TT for you," said Angel, waving the magazine in her hand.

Eli turned round and grinned at her.

"Mrs Chapple. Hello! Just trying to do a bit of sorting here. Coming in for a cuppa?"

"Not today, thanks. Just wanted to drop this off and see how you and Mary are doing."

"Oh we're fine. Fighting fit." He waded through the sheep and took the news-sheet from Angel, glancing quickly at the back page.

"Looking forward to seeing what Spankr's got to offer this time. Me and Mary had a go at the last one. We tried it after I'd finished disinfecting the sheep's feet. Mary had just taken a loaf out of the oven so we had a slice and a nice cup of tea and then Mary suggested we give it a go before I went to sort out some silage. Crackin' it was, I can tell you! Best so far!"

"I'm very glad."

"I hope this one's as good."

"Well, let me know, won't you?" said Angel.

"That I will."

Angel left him to his sheep.

Mark looked up as Angel closed the back door behind her. She kicked off her boots and left them on the mat. Banjo headed straight to his water bowl. Angel put the kettle on before she sat down opposite her husband at the kitchen table. The dog finally settled under her chair. "How was your walk?"

"Fine. What are you up to?"

"Doing the accounts. Seeing if I can find any spare money anywhere to replace the car. And the answer's no. It's going to have to rattle on for a good while yet."

"Won't the church help? They should pay for things like that. After all, you're using it mostly on their behalf."

"It doesn't quite work like that."

"Well it should."

Mark sighed and took off his glasses. He rubbed his eyes wearily.

"Tell me about your walk. Much more interesting."

Angel made them both a cup of coffee and sat back down. "Nothing to tell. It was stunning up on top of the Downs. You could see for miles today. And I saw Eli. He told me that he and Mary had a go at Spankr's last recommendation. Said it was a lot of fun."

Mark put his glasses back on and looked at his wife severely.

"I really don't think you should be printing that sort of stuff you know. It's degrading. Tacky."

"It's harmless, Mark. And quite a few people in the village get a lot out of it. It doesn't hurt anyone."

"I'm not sure about that."

"The postman didn't even know what it was," said Angel.

"Why am I not surprised? He's always been one sheep short of a flock, as they say round here."

Angel smiled at the thought. "He may not be the brightest in the pack but he is kind-hearted. Anyway it's unlike you to be so disapproving."

"I just don't like it, that's all. I think you should stop."

"But you were the one who said what a good idea it was that I started the magazine."

Her husband nodded. "I did, I agree. But that was when it was telling people about important things in the village that would affect them. But not this tawdry stuff you're promoting."

Angel sipped her coffee and sat back. The last thing she wanted was another full-scale argument.

"It's not tawdry. It's not even as if it's explicit, Mark. People can read into it what they will. Spankr's words are whatever you want them to be. They're only suggesting something rude if you think they are. And at the end of the day it's a bit of a laugh and it brightens up a lot of people's lives."

"People like Eli?" Mark sounded incredulous.

"People like Eli. He and Mary get a real buzz out of it."

"They're in their 80s for goodness sake!"

"And your point?"

"Well, it's not natural, is it? People of their age doing things like that!"

"For heaven's sake, Mark, what's got into you these days? What does it matter what age they are? And I bet they get more out of life than we do!"

"What's that supposed to mean?"

"Nothing." Angel knew she had gone too far.

Mark scowled at her. "All I'm saying is that it doesn't look good for the vicar's wife to be touting stuff like that. You shouldn't be putting it in the magazine."

"But that would be censorship. Who am I to say what's included and what isn't?"

"You really have no idea who he is, this Spankr?"

"Who says it's a he?"

"Of course it is. No woman would write something like that."

"Something like what?" asked Angel.

"Like that!" His voice was raised.

"The writer is anonymous," replied Angel emphatically. "Whoever's doing it is dropping it through the letter box. There's no signature so it could be anybody in the village. Somebody in your congregation even. Now there's food for thought! Maybe it's Mrs Strang from Hawthorn Cottage. She looks well up for it. Or better yet, the old vet, Jaspal. Or perhaps it could be Arthur, who does the church flowers. I always thought he was a bit of a dark horse. Or maybe it's all of them!"

"You're talking nonsense and you know it!"

But Angel was on a roll. "Or maybe it's not anyone from Tickbourne at all. Maybe it's someone from further afield. Barrowminster even! They're a strange lot down there." She paused. "Or maybe it's the Bishop!" she suggested wickedly.

Mark stood up. "All I'm asking, Angela, is that you stop including this Spankr bit in the parish magazine. It has no place there. It is offensive and belittles all your good work!"

"No Mark, I don't think it does. I'm not going to censor it. If someone takes the time to write a small contribution to the village newsletter about something which is totally harmless and brings a smile to the faces of most of the villagers, then I am not going to censor it. That's just not going to happen! I have always included everything that anyone sends me and I'm going to continue to do so whether you approve or not!"

"This is not the end of the matter, Angela. Far from it."

Angel looked at her husband. She knew he was cross when he called her by her full name. She put her hands on her hips. "Too damn right, it's not the end of the matter!" And she stormed out of the kitchen, Banjo at her heels.

Angel's suggestion, however nonsensical, that this Spankr might be somebody in his congregation was worrying Mark. What if she was right? What if it was one of his parishioners, sitting there every Sunday, following his every word (as he liked to believe), who was writing this stuff and dropping it into the vicarage letterbox for his wife to publish? No! It was too preposterous. He knew his flock well. They were all honest, straightforward folk, good people who would never do a thing like this. No, somebody was causing mischief, mocking the newsletter and its true purpose and, worse, his wife was complicit. And anyway, what sort of word was Spankr? Mark had no time for this trendy new way of doing things. Dropping letters willy-nilly. In his book you called a spade a spade. Although should that be spad, he mused. And God forbid! What if the Bishop got to hear of it? That must never happen. Mark decided he needed to seek out the culprit as soon as possible and put an end to these salacious scribblings once and for all. As a start, this Sunday he would scan his congregation with eagle eyes, boring into the soul of each and every one of them, looking for anyone who averted their gaze. He had no doubt whatsoever that no such person would exist, having every faith in all his church members. But if anyone couldn't look him in the eye, well, that would be pause for thought. When he got a minute he'd have a look at all the back copies of the Tickbourne Tattler and see exactly what this Spankr had written. There might be some clues there as to his identity. Mark was convinced it could only be a man. Meanwhile he had a sermon to write.

Angel had started the Tickbourne Tattler shortly after she and Mark first arrived in the village. For the first time since her marriage to Mark, her life was not fully occupied with his church matters. For once she had time on her hands, there being very little for her to do in the village, so she'd mooted the idea to her husband that a monthly newsletter would be good for the residents and would help her fill her time. Having come from a desperately busy inner-city parish of the deprived and much-neglected city of Harmley, where she'd been engaged in all sorts of work supportive of her husband's role - holding coffee mornings to raise funds for disenfranchised market gardeners; running the inappropriately named after-school club for truants; organising jumble sales and cake-bakes as part of the Halt Hunger in Harmley campaign, Tickbourne had been, and still very much was, a breath of fresh air. Both she and Mark had been more than happy to quit city life.

Mark was burned out. So much to do and so little money, he felt as if he could never make a difference to people's lives, something he believed was his mission in life. Angel had found the constant whingeing and whining of her husband's parishioners enervating. Yes, life could be hard, she told herself, but you needed to make the most of what you had, no matter how little. But even that dogma was put to the test daily as Angel had to contend with their poky second floor flat overlooking the railway lines, with its rising damp and ever-present smell of drains. The lift had never worked from the day they moved in and, despite the church promising them it was to be a temporary home, they were there for over 10 years, the entire length of Mark's inner-city tenure. The few green spaces in Harmley featured discarded needles, used condoms and abandoned furniture. There was nowhere for Angel to breathe and her natural optimism for life was slowly eroded over the years. Everything was centred around Mark and his work and Angel increasingly felt as if she were merely his side-kick and that any contribution she made was worthless. She found herself subject to uncharacteristic and quite frightening dark moods. Exhausted, she felt as if she was drowning, being smothered. So when Mark, finally recognising that they both needed a change, mentioned that a post in the rural village of Tickbourne had been advertised in Venues for Vicars, she Googled it. Having discovered the village was in the middle of nowhere she begged her husband to apply immediately. He needed little persuasion and within weeks they were told the living was theirs. And perhaps, thought Angel, such a move might even put a little something back into their jaded marriage. God knows, they needed it.

Within two months Mark and Angel had moved into their new home. A small vicarage, it was true, but the lack of size was more than made up for by the location and the peace and quiet. Their new home overlooked the church and its graveyard and the only noise that kept them awake at nights now was the hooting of owls in the nearby copse. No more police or ambulance sirens shattered their peace. No-one knocked on their flat door in the early hours of the morning, requiring their presence to sort out their latest catastrophe. As far as Angel was concerned, Tickbourne was not only a taste of paradise, it was a life-saver. She fell in love with the village, its residents and her new way of life. And now, with no meetings to organise, no funds to raise, no emergencies to deal with, she looked for other outlets to occupy her time. The creation of a parish magazine was an obvious choice.

Despite the fact that the Tickbourne Tattler had been going for a good few years now, it was only in the last six months that Spankr had made its first appearance. She remembered it well. The newsletter was almost ready to print but there was a gap on the back page and try as she might, she couldn't re-configure the text to fill the space. She needed something, an infill. But what? She'd already included a small item from Mrs Apis offering jars of her honey for a small donation to the Cats' Comfort charity. Angel had managed to include a drawing of a bee hovering over a dandelion - she was quietly proud of her artwork - but she needed something more. Another possible contribution found its way into the letterbox. This time it was from Major Works (Retd.) in the form of a letter asking people to stop letting their dogs shit all over the water meadows. He was tired of exercising Millie, his Pointer, amongst other animals' turds. Angel, despite her professed reluctance to censor anything that was submitted, thought the language would need toning down and this was something she could not bring herself to do. Spankr provided the solution. And fortunately it fitted perfectly.

The first notice was a huge success;

> I'm Spankr. Make of me what you will. I aim to make your life more adventurous. More fun. This is for adults with a sense of humour and a passion to play. Each month I will suggest something which will brighten your day and benefit your body and soul. Interpret it however you choose but always with an open mind. Explore! Be bold! If I say 'Pushing the Tush', think outside the box. Your imagination should know no bounds.

Angel read it over and over but couldn't see any harm in it. After all, what did the message really say? She knew it had fruity overtones and was mildly suggestive - the name alone was a bit of a give-away - but it promised to benefit the villagers so surely only good could come of it? Should she run it past her husband? No. Mark had always said the parish magazine was hers and hers alone so Angel decided to go ahead and print. And that was it. After Pushing the Tush came The Maharajah, The Speed Bump, The Pearly Gates, Frighten the Pigeon, and last month's recommendation, A Peal of Bells. At first there was much head scratching in the village and some puzzled exchanges over a pint in the Heron Fancier, but after a few weeks Spankr's message gradually became clear to all. The villagers did as they were told and used their imagination. Suddenly the population of Tickbourne had a big collective smile on its face and some new and unexpected friendships were being forged. People would stop each other in the street (all except Matthew the Postman who, of course, just didn't get it), to compare notes as to how they'd interpreted Spankr's latest suggestion. And each month the residents of this sleepy little village waited eagerly for Angel to deliver their copy of the Tattler which would bring some new excitement into their once-staid lives. There was great conjecture amongst them as to who Spankr was. Each and every resident vehemently denied that they were the author whilst secretly rather wishing that they were. There was even speculation that it was the vicar's wife herself but this idea was immediately rejected. Not Angel. No. Maybe it was the vicar who was the author of these suggestions? Whoever it was the Fleas decided, singly and universally, it didn't matter. Spankr brought a spark to their often dull lives and for that they were grateful. The only person who was very definitely not amused by Spankr and his offerings was the vicar himself.

Mark Chapple finally lost it one Sunday morning just after he'd finished his sermon - a discourse on the need for open-mindedness and generosity in our daily dealings with the people around us and the importance of leading by example. He happened to catch his wife's eye as he spoke. Angel raised an eyebrow. Really? He stumbled over his text, reminding himself of his earlier comments about Spankr and the elderly farmer, Eli and his wife, Mary. The vicar coughed, red-faced, then continued, announcing that before blessing the congregation and letting them go home for their Sunday roasts he had several important notices to read out. Volunteers were needed to help with the annual weeding of the graveyard; the ladies who ran the knitting group, the Purl and Parl, in the vestry each week were reminded to take away any uneaten biscuits as the mice infestation had clearly returned; and finally, to celebrate Mrs Titian's 95th birthday, a peal of bells would ring out at midday tomorrow. A huge roar of laughter greeted this last announcement. The vicar was confused. What was so funny?

Then he recalled Spankr's most recent suggestion. He glared at the assembled company, his wife included.

"I will not have this frivolity in the church!" he shouted at them. "This is a sacred place, not a house of mirth!"

The assembly fell silent, suitably admonished. But that, at least, answered a question. Spankr was clearly not the vicar, then. Mark Chapple scanned the pews slowly, looking at each and every one of his congregation in turn. Not a single member could meet his eye. This is worse than I thought, he decided. Something would have to be done. But what? Forgetting to bless his parishioners, he climbed slowly down from the pulpit and instead of heading to the church door as he usually would, to shake the hands of the members of his congregation as they left the church, he walked into the vestry, his head bowed. Angel wasn't going to abandon Spankr if it was the last thing she did.

That evening, Mark sat at the kitchen table, his spaghetti carbonara cold and uneaten in front of him.

"You can't blame them," said Angel. "They didn't mean anything."

"I don't blame them. I blame you!" he snarled. "They made a mockery of me. Just as you have."

Angel was indignant. "I am not mocking you! I never have and I never will."

"You're mocking my beliefs. You and your bloody Spankr!"

Angel stared at him. This was the first time she had ever heard her husband swear.

"It's an abomination and you've converted the entire village into a whole load of perverts!" he ranted.

"Perverts? I have done nothing of the sort! It's just a bit of fun."

"So you keep saying!" He twirled a bit of spaghetti on his fork then threw it down in disgust. "How can I ever preach to them again? How can I ever look them in the eye when I know what they're thinking? You don't know what you've done!"

"I haven't done anything, Mark." Angel was trying to stay calm.

"You are my wife," he reminded her unnecessarily. "We're expected to sing from the same hymn sheet, in every respect!"

Angel couldn't help a smile.

"I'm expected to lead by example," Mark continued. "Now you've embarrassed me! In front of my parishioners. What am I to do?"

"What are you to do? Why, nothing. You carry on doing what you've always done. You're their vicar and they respect you." She was going to say adore but thought that was taking it a bit too far.

"Not any more they don't, thanks to you."

Angel stood up and cleared his plate away. "You're over-exaggerating, Mark. This Spankr thing is just a bit of harmless fun."

"Harmless fun? You don't know the half of it. Look!" From his trouser pocket he pulled a crumpled envelope.

"What is it?"

"It's a letter from the Bishop. That's what that is! It came last week. He's coming here tomorrow. He wants to discuss some issues he's been made aware of. That can only mean Spankr."

Angel picked up the envelope and removed the letter. She sat down as she read it then put it down on the table.

"I'm finished here," said Mark. "Finished as a vicar."

"It doesn't say that."

"It doesn't have to."

Angel reached over and put her hand on her husband's. Angrily he pulled his away.

"All you have to do is to tell him it's my fault. You told me the magazine was my responsibility. Mine and mine alone. It's got nothing to do with you. Problem solved."

"You just don't get it, do you?"

Angel tried one last time to reason with him. "Look, Mark, the Bishop is only human. He might even see the funny side of it."

Her husband stared at her in disbelief. "Okay. Maybe he won't. But even if he doesn't there's nothing salacious in the newsletter. I wouldn't have put it there if it was. You read into it what you will. None of the villagers are complaining. In fact, I've never seen them happier. Or healthier. And no-one's being forced into anything they don't want to do. It's a matter of personal choice."

Mark folded his arms. "I refuse to discuss it any more. I just want you to know that I hold you personally responsible for my downfall."

"Isn't that being just a wee bit dramatic?"

"I don't think so. I can never forgive you, Angela, for what you've done."

Angel sat back in her chair, noting the demotion again from a heavenly being to a mere mortal.

"Okay."

"Okay? Is that all you've got to say?" For someone who didn't want to discuss the matter, Mark obviously still considered there was more to be said.

"It is. You won't listen to me, so there's no point saying anything else."

Mark stood. "I'm going out for a walk. I'll take the dog with me. At least he still has some respect for me!"

Angel re-read the Bishop's letter. The issues were unspecified but she had no doubt her husband was right. It could only be about Spankr. Would Mark be sacked? Or worse still, banished? Would they be sent back to the hell and damnation that was inner-city

Harmley as punishment for her crime? That was something she couldn't face. But didn't the Church do redemption? Wasn't it all supposed to be about forgiveness? And anyway, what was her crime? As far as Angel was concerned she, and Spankr, had done the village a favour. The residents were happy, contented, and had a vicar they liked and respected, whatever Mark thought. Spankr had brought a new dimension to the lives of many, clearly enlivening what could have been a long and lonely old age for the majority of the Fleas. She and Mark should get a reward not a condemnation. Together they had made Tickbourne their home and they'd done it proud. No, she couldn't face moving away. Her life was here. This was her sanctuary.

Angel had only met the Bishop once, when her husband was ordained. She remembered being surprised at how young he'd looked at the time, always imagining Bishops to be grey and bent. He had been perfectly pleasant to her on that occasion, to both of them, and then she had put him out of her mind whilst they got on with her husband's calling. Would he still be as pleasant? Or would the bringer of bad news, ending her life as she knew it, look more like a devil in disguise? It wasn't only be Mark who didn't sleep well that night.

───※───

Angel knew when she woke from a disturbed and restless sleep that a Rubicon had been crossed yesterday. Her husband's accusations had hurt her. He'd never spoken to her like that before. Their marriage, whilst hardly exciting, had been one more of companionship than anything else. Grand passions were for other people, she'd long since realised. She and Mark had rumbled along together over the years, rarely arguing, seldom a raised voice, and it had worked for them both. Maybe children would have made a difference. She doubted it. Mark was too involved with his Church to have time for children and Angel would probably have had to have brought them up on her own. Easier not to have bothered. She had no regrets and from what she could tell, neither did her husband. But if Mark were to lose his job, to be decommissioned as it were, there would be regrets aplenty. And after what he'd said yesterday, blaming her in full for what he called his downfall, those regrets were apparently already starting to seep in.

The Bishop was due at lunchtime. Angel couldn't decide what to cook but decided to keep it simple. Today would be pivotal for her and Mark, one way or another, so their very own Last Supper might as well be one of their favourites. As she defrosted some salmon from the freezer, she made a blackberry crumble using last year's berries from the graveyard. Angel popped one of their few 'special occasion' bottles of wine in the fridge. They might need it. She was on her own in the kitchen, Mark having disappeared first thing in the morning into the church, muttering something about things needing fixing. It was better that way - she couldn't think of a single thing she wanted to say to him. At 12 o'clock sharp the Bishop parked his Mercedes outside the vicarage. Mark suddenly appeared as if he had been on the lookout for his boss' arrival. He had. The usual courtesies exchanged, Mark showed his visitor round the small church and its graveyard. Theirs was generally small-talk - life in general; the late arrival of spring; but more importantly for them both, the difficulties of maintaining interest and hence congregations, in the church in a modern world. Lunch was a pleasant enough affair, though Mark was clearly a nervous wreck throughout the entire meal, toying with his food and eating little. The Bishop, however, tucked in to both food and wine but there was still no mention of the issues. It was over coffee in the lounge that the matter was finally broached.

"Thank you for a wonderful meal. Simply divine!" The Bishop laughed at his own joke. "You would not believe how many formal dinners I have to go to and all the posh stuff I have to eat. I can't go anywhere without my Rennies these days! No, you can't beat simple food well done. I congratulate you, Angela."

"Thank you," Angel smiled at him. He has aged beautifully, she thought.

"It is truly delightful here," he said, leaning back in his armchair, burping quietly. "So peaceful. Very different from Harmley. I can't imagine you would want to leave. I know I wouldn't." He stood up and went to the window, sighing as he looked out across the graveyard.

Mark crossed and uncrossed his legs. "You said there were some issues you wanted to raise."

The Bishop turned. "Oh yes. Of course. Almost forgot the reason I came!" He sat back down. "I almost hate what I'm going to say. It's come to my attention..."

Two stomachs somersaulted, one more than the other.

"...that someone called Spankr is writing in your parish magazine."

Mark felt sick.

"Has there been a complaint?" asked Angel nervously.

"A complaint? Oh no. My secretary pointed it out to me. He reads all the parish magazines for me. Helps keep me grounded. A complaint? No, far from it. He tells me - and I've heard it from other sources too - that the parishioners of Tickbourne are some of the happiest in my diocese, if not the entire land! If only all my other parishes were like this."

Mark and Angel looked at each other, mouths open.

"Whatever you're both doing, and Spankr, of course, you're working a miracle."

"So Spankr's not a problem?" asked Angel tentatively

"Far from it. Every parish should have one!"

"Then why did you say that you hated what you were about to say?" asked Mark, relieved but confused.

"Well, since you have both done such sterling work here, I'm going to offer you a promotion, Mark. Bigger and better things. My concern is dragging you both away from this idyll."

"I don't know what to say," said Mark. "I thought you wouldn't approve of Spankr."

"Why ever not? I am human, after all. And, to be honest, he's given me a few ideas I can tell you! There! I bet that surprised you. Yes, whoever Spankr is - do you have any idea at all?" Both Mark and Angel shook their heads. "Shame. Well, whoever he, or she, is, they have brightened an awful lot of lives."

Angel stared hard at her husband.

"When you say promotion, what exactly are you talking about?" Mark asked the Bishop.

"I'm looking at you taking over several parishes. Big ones. As a Rector. There'd be a salary increase. And bigger premises of course, though I can't imagine anything more delightful than this. There's a vacancy coming up down south. In Rotchester, to be exact. City living again, I'm afraid, but nothing like Harmley. What do you say?"

Mark looked at his wife, a smile stretching from ear to ear. Having long recovered from his burnout in Harmley he'd decided he was ready for another challenge. And this was it. He suddenly realised this was what he'd been waiting for. But Angel did not smile back.

"I don't know what to say!" beamed Mark.

"Well, think about it," said the Bishop, standing. "I don't need an answer yet. The end of the week will do."

He shook hands with his hosts. "Thank you again for a lovely lunch. I'll see myself out."

Confessions

"Can you believe that?" Mark was clearly dumbfounded.

"That was the last thing I expected. I really thought I was going to be sacked."

"I told you there was nothing to worry about. Spankr is completely harmless. In fact, he's done you a favour."

"As have you. I'm really sorry about what I said."

"So am I," replied Angel. "It was pretty hurtful. And untrue."

"I know and I shouldn't have said it. But all I could see was my hard work here, and especially all my efforts in Harmley, being all for nothing."

"My efforts too," she reminded him.

"Of course. Yours too. But think what this means for us. Things have been a bit off-kilter between us recently but this will be a new start. We'll be able to afford a few more luxuries. Maybe even a holiday. A bigger place to live. Sure, it's more responsibility for me but I won't mind that. I'm ready for another challenge again. Oh, Angel, I'm so excited! I can hardly wait. And Rotchester of all places."

Angel got up and went into the kitchen, retrieved the wine bottle from the fridge and poured herself a glass. Taking a large swallow she returned to the lounge to face her husband.

"I'm not going," she said simply.

"What? What do you mean?"

"I mean I'm not going with you to Rotchester. I'm staying here."

"But why? I mean, you can't. You've got to come with me. You're my wife."

"I can't see that that has any bearing on the matter. I'm staying here. This is my home and I'm not leaving it."

Mark looked alarmed. "But we can make Rotchester our new home. You'd like that, wouldn't you?" He was almost pleading.

Angel shook her head. "No, Mark, I wouldn't."

"But why ever not? What's brought all this on?"

"You want this promotion. Another challenge. I don't. I don't want to move from here. This is the only place I ever want to be."

"You're being obtuse. And stupid."

Angel shrugged her shoulders. "Am I? I love this place, Mark, and I'm not going to leave it."

"You love this place more than you love me?"

"Yes. I'm afraid I do."

"But I don't understand. How can you love a place more than a person? It doesn't make any sense. Don't you want to be with me?"

Angel shook her head. "No. Not any more."

"But what have I done?"

How long have you got? Angel thought to herself. She took another drink.

"Mark, I put up with all those dreadful years in Harmley and hated every single day there. 10 years of my life. Wasted. And you just accepted that I would be there. By your side. And I was. I supported you and your work. But never once did you ask what I wanted. If I was happy. It was only when you realised that you needed a change that the thought of moving out of Harmley even crossed your mind. And then when we moved here I was happy. Truly happy, for the first time in years. I fell in love with Tickbourne and I want to stay here."

"That's utterly selfish," he snarled.

"No more so than you've been. You can go ahead and tell the Bishop that you are going to accept the promotion but that I won't be coming with you."

"Do the past 13 years mean nothing to you? Does our marriage not mean anything?"

Angel thought before she spoke. "It did. But there has to be more. For me."

Mark put his head in his hands. "You can't mean it, Angel. Please. I'm begging you. Come with me."

Angel finished the wine in her glass. "I'm sorry, Mark. But I can't."

"What would it take to make you come with me? There must be something?"

"There isn't. My mind's made up."

"But where will you live? What will you do?"

"I really don't know. But I'll manage. Banjo and me. We'll be fine. And anyway, I'm sure the parishioners will look after me. After all, they owe me."

"Owe you? What are you talking about?"

Angel smiled. "Well, I'm the one who's brought a little bit more excitement into their humdrum lives. I spiced things up for them. Made their retirement a wee bit more fun."

Mark stared at her incredulously. "You don't mean it? Tell me you're not Spankr?"

She nodded.

"But how? You said the contributions were anonymous. They just turned up in our letterbox."

"They were anonymous. I never put my name or anyone else's to them. And as for being dropped in the letterbox. A little white lie on my part. So no harm done."

"No harm done! You have wrecked our marriage with your sordid little ways!"

Angel raised one eyebrow. "Wrecked our marriage? I don't think so," she said calmly. "I think you can lay claim to that honour all on your own. And besides, Spankr has got you the promotion you so badly wanted. So everyone's happy."

"I can never forgive you, you know that," said Mark bitterly.

Angel stood up. "I don't need you to. I can live happily without your forgiveness. And I will." She headed towards the kitchen. "Go and make your phone call, Mark. It's time for a change."

2
FIVE PAST SOUTHAMPTON

"How would I go about finding a stripper?"

"What?" Derek choked on his tea. "A stripper? Why on earth would you want a stripper?"

"Not for me, you idiot! It's for Josh. For his birthday."

Derek put his mug down on the coffee table. "Have I missed something here, Sam?"

Sam stirred another teaspoon of sugar into his mug.

"I just thought, it's a big birthday, it might be a nice idea to surprise him."

"Surprise him?" asked Derek. "I think it's more likely you'll give the poor bugger a heart attack! How old is he anyway? I know he's a lot younger than the rest of us."

"He'll be 60 next birthday."

Derek shook his head in disbelief. "60, eh? That's no age. But still, as you say, a big one. What do you think, Ravi?"

"I'm not sure I can remember when I was 60," Ravi laughed. "Seems like a lifetime ago and to all intents and purposes, it practically is."

"But what do you think about getting a stripper?" Derek asked him again.

"I'm not sure to be honest. I don't like the idea of exploiting women."

"Good point," agreed Derek.

"Well we could get a what do you call 'em? An ecologically-sourced one."

Derek and Ravi stared at Sam incredulously.

"What?" they said simultaneously.

"I don't mean that, do I?" Sam shook his head. "No, what I mean is we could get one who likes her job. Does it for fun."

"I can't see anyone taking their clothes off for fun," said Ravi.

"More likely it's because they need to put food on the table," suggested Derek.

"We should ask Trevor. See what he thinks. Speaking of which, where is he? He should be here by now. We did say 10.30, didn't we?"

"We did. And Josh is late too," Derek pointed out.

At that moment the front doorbell rang.

For the past eight years the four widowers, Sam, Derek, Ravi and Trevor, had been meeting up every Monday and Thursday - unless one of them had some unalterable medical appointment, or, very occasionally but far less likely, one of their offspring (remote in every sense of the word), required their presence at some family gathering. More often than not this was for a grandchild's birthday - for those that had them - or some other compelling celebration. More usually, it was a means to attempt to persuade their aged father to part with some more money, a small loan, just to tide them over. These twice-weekly gatherings of the four men were the backbone of their lives. All of them were long-since retired, all pretty much on their own, and this was the only real social life they had. Here was true companionship, something to look forward to. When they'd first started meeting up it had been in a cafe on the High Street but when that closed down, probably partly due to the fact that they spent half the morning there with only a few coffees and the odd packet of biscuits to sustain them, Derek had offered them the use of his house. They'd jumped at the opportunity and it had been their meeting place ever since, apart from the one occasion when his bathroom had flooded bringing down the kitchen ceiling. During the two weeks Derek's house was out of action, with a succession of plasterers and plumbers doing their bit, the four convened at Sam's, but it wasn't as convenient or as pleasant. For one thing, it wasn't as central - Derek's house had the advantage of being on most of the major bus routes (although Ravi always chose to drive). Nor did Sam's house possess everything else that Derek's had to offer - a large comfortable lounge overlooking a splendidly maintained garden (Derek paid for someone to make it look that good), a downstairs toilet and, most importantly, there was always cake. Derek was not short of a bob or two, his friends knew, his pensions and careful investments having secured him a comfortable retirement, so he always ensured that he provided at least three cakes of the finest quality money could buy to offer his companions. Having been a master baker in his younger days, there was a time when he would have baked them himself. Now, arthritis limiting his dexterity and stamina in the kitchen, he bought them from a local bakery just down the road. They were nowhere near as good as the ones he'd once made, he never failed to tell his friends smugly, but they were the best that money could buy in Portsmouth. All poor Sam could stretch to was the odd packet of Chocolate Cartwheels which they ate whilst seated cheek by jowl round his tiny kitchen table; and what with that and the awkward and usually frequent climb upstairs to the cold and draughty bathroom, Sam's place was far from ideal. No, Derek's was the preferred venue and everyone was more than happy with the arrangement. They each pretty much planned their entire lives around the gatherings. It was a chance to spend time with friends, an opportunity to put the world to rights. To rail against the government, the council, Portsmouth FC (as far as Derek was concerned), and life in general. They'd drifted together over the years although Derek and Trevor had known each other on and off since schooldays. It was their widower status and their loneliness that drew them together and for all of them their get-togethers were what made the world go round.

Then, six months ago, unexpectedly, there was a new addition to the group. Josh joined them. And the four became five.

It was Sam who'd first met Josh. After one Thursday meeting at Derek's, Sam had decided to stop off at his local pub, The Articulate Angler, just round the corner from his house. He wasn't keen to get home - he never was. His poky two-up two-down was shabby and unwelcoming. It was always cold and damp even in the height of summer and he hated the place. But it was all he could afford after paying the care home bills for Louise, his wife of 45 years. Unable to cope with the increasing demands of her dementia he'd had to sell their home to pay for someone who could. At the time it was yet another stab in the heart; not only was he slowly losing the love of his life but more quickly, he lost the wonderful home they'd shared their entire marriage. His heart had broken completely. And this tiny Victorian terraced house on a street of similar grim houses was his only option, the care home fees having bled him dry over the years. Sam was so pleased Louise had never seen it. She would have hated it. It was the opposite of everything their marital home had been. Dingy and rundown, it was a shell, empty of everything that made it a place you wanted to spend any time. There hadn't even been enough money left after Louise had died to get the place spruced up so it remained as cheerless and uninviting as the day he'd moved in. He'd furnished it with second hand bits and pieces he'd picked up from charity shops and car boot sales; a rickety kitchen table, mismatching chairs, a couple of sagging armchairs. He'd been given an old gas cooker by a neighbour who'd taken pity on him and he'd found a fridge in a skip. He soon came to regret the latter. What he thought at the time was a stroke of luck turned out to be a nightmare as the fridge was temperamental, apparently with a mind of its own. It either produced copious amounts of ice or flooded the kitchen floor, depending on what sort of mood it was in. There was no money to replace it - his pension barely covered the essentials. This is living, Sam, he told himself many a time, but not as we know it. The only good thing he could say about the house was that it was his and no-one could take it away from him. Not that anyone would want to, he thought ruefully.

Having had no children and with no other family, Sam was alone. Many was the night he sat in front of his tv, staring mindlessly at the flickering screen. He tried to recall how good life had been for him, for them both. But then he'd remember how it had all gone downhill when Louise started to disappear. Little things at first; she'd begin to do something, boil a kettle or make a sandwich, then wander off, leaving the job half done. Then getting dressed in the mornings started to become problematical for her. Soon after that, some of the things she said no longer made any sense - well, not to him at least. Sam finally realised they needed help when one night Louise got up to use the bathroom and didn't come back. He'd found the front door wide open, rain soaking the carpet. He'd phoned the police immediately. They'd found her, drenched and shivering violently, sitting on a bench overlooking the harbour, singing quietly to herself. Louise had walked miles in her bare feet dressed only in her nightie, oblivious to the cold and wet. And from then on she remained oblivious to pretty much everything. Including Sam. The man with whom she had spent 45 years of her life. He was a stranger to her and that hurt him more than words could say.

When Derek's place was flooded and temporarily out of action for their meetings, Sam felt obliged to offer his home as an alternative venue. Ravi's place, way over the other side of town, was do-able but it would take three buses; and Trevor lived with his aged mum, so that was a non-starter. That only left Sam's. Against his better judgement Sam had offered to host their meetings until Derek's place dried out. But he had never been more embarrassed in his whole life. Of course, his friends had said nothing. They were gentlemen after all. But he'd cringed every time he'd opened his front door to them. He was used to the overpowering smell of damp and mould, the peeling wallpaper, the stained and worn carpets. They were not and he'd felt utterly humiliated as he'd welcomed them to his very, very humble home. He vowed then that should Derek's place ever flood again he would not be repeating the offer.

Yes, he said to himself, a drink at the pub would, once again, happily delay his return home. The place was warm, the landlord friendly and for a few hours at least, he could forget the emptiness that was always waiting for him.

The Articulate Angler had stood on the corner of Empire Street and Harbour Road since the year dot though the name had changed many times over the years. Once infamous for its press gangs, recruiting unwilling and usually highly inebriated victims to sail the seven seas, it was now home to the more mundane weekly Pie and Peas Extravaganza and the fortnightly Quiz Night. Sam usually availed himself of both - anything to delay his return home. He pushed the door open and was hit by a wall of heat combined with stale odours of sweet beer and sour sweat. He smiled as he drank in the welcoming atmosphere. The décor was nothing to write home about; everything was brown - it was just a question of degree. The walls and ceilings were a uniformly-stained shade of nicotine and the reassuringly sticky carpet, whose pattern had long since faded, was of a darker hue. All the furniture was dark brown, whether the banquettes that lined the walls or the wooden chairs that clustered round the mismatching tables. These were their own indescribable shade of brown, verging on black, and you could guarantee that anything you might place on one of these tables, pint glass, dominoes, elbow, would never slide off such was the adhesive nature of their surface. The place hadn't had a lick of paint in years; Charlie, the landlord, could see little point in wasting good money on redecorating - he firmly believed this was what his clientele liked and that suited him fine. Sam loved the place.

"The usual?" Charlie asked him as Sam approached the bar. Sam nodded, watching as the landlord pulled him a pint of Partly Cloudy. He sipped the beer then turned round. It was still early but the pub was almost half full. He recognised most of the patrons and nodded to one or two of them but he was intrigued by a man he'd never seen before, sitting alone at a table in the corner. He was shabbily dressed in a threadbare jacket and jeans. The man had a pint in front of him but it was untouched. He sat, staring into the past. For some reason, which Sam could never have explained, he felt the urge to go and talk to the man.

"Mind if I join you, mate?"

The man looked up.

"What? I mean, yes, of course. If you want."

Sam sat down opposite him.

"Sam," he said, proffering his hand.

The man shook it reluctantly, unhappy at being disturbed. "Josh."

Sam raised his glass. "Josh."

Josh, with some difficulty, prised his glass from the table. They clinked glasses. And that, as they say, was the start of what they hoped would be a beautiful friendship.

But before Josh could join the group the unanimous approval of the members was required. It had always been the four of them right from the start; Derek, Ravi, Sam and Trevor, and Sam's suggestion that they swell their ranks to five was met with mixed feelings. No-one had ever suggested before that someone new join them - this would take some careful consideration.

"But what do we know about him?" asked Trevor.

"Well," replied Sam, "he's on his own. He's lonely. And he's sad. Isn't that enough?"

"In principle, yes. But it's always been just the four of us. And we've known each other for years. We're all widowers. All on our lonesomes, as it were. Is he?"

"Very much so. He told me he was all alone and had been for a very long time." Sam told the others at great length how he'd spotted Josh sitting alone in the pub, looking bereft. He recounted how Josh had told him that he had no-one and nothing in his life now that his wife was gone. At first Josh had been reluctant to talk but with a little persuasion from Sam, coupled with a few more beers, he began to open up. And once he started he couldn't stop. It was if he'd been waiting for someone with whom he could share his story, his isolation. When Sam had stood up to go, Josh had reached over and clasped his hands. Can we meet again? he'd asked. Please? So Sam had agreed to meet Josh the following afternoon and the afternoon after that. Josh had poured out his heart, telling him that once his wife had gone, his friends had disappeared too. Never had Sam come across anyone who needed to unburden himself so much and his heart went out to the man. Josh had told him that he had been something in the printing business - newspapers - all his working life. He'd met the love of his life, Margot, when they were just 16 and they'd married two years later. They'd had no children but it didn't matter. They'd revelled in each other's company and couldn't bear to be apart from each other, not for a moment. But now they were. Poor Josh was devastated. He'd wiped a tear from his eye, Sam recounted. And I did too, he admitted to the others. What the man needs is companions. Friends to help him get through the dark days.

"Well, I suppose you'd better invite him round," said Derek. "We'll have chat. See if he'll fit."

Trevor nodded. "Yes, it's very important that we all get on with him. How old did you say he was?"

"He's only 59."

"That's a lot younger than any of us," said Ravi. "He might be too young."

"Can you be too young to suffer pain and loss?" Sam asked with surprising vehemence. "Is there an age limit on loneliness?"

"No, of course there isn't. You're absolutely right, Sam. Bring him round next Thursday," suggested Derek. "I'm sure he'll fit in perfectly."

Sam and Josh had met outside the pub the following Thursday morning. They walked in silence to the nearby bus stop and waited patiently for the 415.

"I must admit I'm nervous," said Josh, smiling weakly. "What if they don't like me?"

"Don't be daft. There's no need for that sort of talk," replied Sam. "They're a great bunch of guys. Real good friends. You'll like them. I know you will."

"But will they like me?"

"Of course they will. you'll be fine. Stop worrying,"

Some 30 minutes later they stood on Derek's doorstep.

"Here we are," announced Sam. "Derek's."

Josh looked at the unusual painted wooden plaque attached to the front door. On a piece of stained oak painted in gold was the house number FIVE and underneath, PAST SOUTHAMPTON.

"What's all that about?"

Sam smiled. "I'll let the man tell you himself."

The door was opened by a smiling Derek.

"Come in! Come in!"

Josh wiped his feet on the doormat whilst pointing to the unusual house name.

"What's this?" he asked.

"That, my dear fellow, was the final result of the South Coast Derby of 1982 when we finally thrashed Southampton 5 - 0. One of the happiest days of my life."

"I remember that," beamed Josh. "It was Routledge, wasn't it, scored three of them? Got the third past the goalie in the last minute of the game."

Sam had never seen him so animated.

Derek looked at the man with new respect. "It was! Were you there?"

"I was. Were you?"

"Too right I was. I used to have a season ticket for Portsmouth. Until standing in the cold for too long did my knees in. Now I just follow them on the telly. But I had to record the score for posterity. What do you think? Five Past Southampton! Did it myself." Derek proudly stroked the sign, his fingers caressing each gold letter and the number 5, over and over. "Big and bold, for all the world to see. What do you think?"

"I think it's brilliant! The best result ever in the history of the club and what a way to celebrate and remind everybody at the same time!"

Sam coughed loudly.

"What? Oh yes! Sorry. Come on in and meet the other guys. They're all here. I can't tell you how thrilled I am to have another Pompey supporter on board! None of the others are even remotely interested in football."

As far as Derek was concerned there was no more to be said. Josh was a shoo-in. How could he not be part of their group? And despite none of the others having anything like the same enthusiasm as their host for 22 allegedly grown men futilely kicking a ball around on a muddy, unbelievably wet pitch in the middle of winter, they all recognised a kindred spirit. He was alone and he was lonely. Josh needed friends. He needed them. He was so young compared with them and to have lost his wife at such a young age was unbearably sad. They'd welcomed him with open arms.

"How do we go about finding a stripper, then?" asked Derek. "It can't be that difficult when you think about it."

"In my day all you had to do was go to a public phone box. One of those old red ones. It was so easy," said Trevor.

"Don't tell me you ever rang one?" asked Ravi.

"Oh no!" Trevor sounded shocked at the idea. "All I'm saying is, that's where you found them." He paused. "If you wanted one," he added as an afterthought.

"You mean you could actually find strippers in a phone box?" laughed Sam. He was struggling with the image.

"No! Their cards. Tart cards, I think they were called. I do miss the passing of phone boxes, don't you? There was all sorts of light reading in there."

"Light reading?"

"The cards, I mean. Stuck to the glass. Every sort of trade you could think of. French lessons. Dance classes. Fortune telling. Chassis Servicing."

"Don't you think they might have all been in the same line of business?" Ravi suggested.

Trevor looked puzzled. "Oh, I don't think so." He scratched his head. "No. Surely not."

"I saw one the other day near the park," said Sam.

"What? A stripper?" asked Ravi.

"No. A phone box. Had one of those things inside."

Ravi, Derek and Trevor looked at him expectantly.

"Go on! Give us a clue," said Trevor.

"You know. That thing for starting your heart."

"A bottle of whisky, you mean?" laughed Ravi.

"No. One of those mechanical things. You know. A defenestrator!"

"You mean a defibrillator," said Trevor.

"Isn't that what I said?"

"Not as such," replied Derek, standing. "More cake anyone? I've got a Lime and Coconut Special in the kitchen."

There were nods all round.

"You have to go online these days to find anything," said Ravi. "Everything's online."

"What if you don't have a computer?" asked Sam. "I don't."

"Libraries have ones you can use. And they'll show you how to use them."

"Oh I can just see that! Going into Portsmouth library and saying, Excuse me Miss - and you can bet your bottom dollar it would be a lady librarian - Can you show me how to use the computer so I can find a stripper?"

"Sam's got a point there," agreed Derek.

"The only problem with searching online is you're going to find yourself bombarded for ever more with all sorts of stuff you don't want or need. There are links to weird sites and adverts for things to solve the problems you didn't even know you had."

Sam looked at Ravi. What was he talking about? As a council-employed carpenter he'd never had the need for a computer and now they were beyond him. If he'd managed 76 years without one, he wasn't going to start now, stripper or no stripper.

"What about a newsagent's?" he asked.

"Good thinking," said Derek. "They have all sorts in their windows. Corner shops too. One of us could go in and ask."

"Not me," said Sam quickly. "I'd be too embarrassed."

"We're all in this together," said Trevor. "It was your suggestion we get Josh a stripper for his birthday. And if we're all in favour of doing that then we all have to get involved in finding one."

"Speaking of Josh," said Derek, suddenly noticing his absence, "why isn't he here?"

"He said something about some root canal work. Sounded painful, whatever it was. Don't you remember?" said Trevor.

Derek nodded. "Oh yes. Anyway, just as well he's not here because if this is to be a surprise, we couldn't very well plan it with him here, could we?"

"Maybe this isn't such a good idea after all." Sam was clearly having doubts.

"Why? What's making you have second thoughts?" asked Ravi.

"I don't know. We've never done anything like this before. Isn't it a bit...tacky?"

"I suppose a lot will depend on who we choose and how it's done," said Trevor. "I understand it can be quite tasteful."

"I actually think it is a good idea," said Derek. "As birthday presents go, it's pretty unique. Should bring a smile to his face. God knows! Something needs to."

"Yes, if there's anyone in need of some serious cheering up, that person is Josh," agreed Trevor. "Poor bugger."

All four men nodded silently.

"What do we think then?" asked Derek. "Should we get him a stripper? We all have to agree. It's all or nothing."

"Should we draw straws?" asked Sam.

"For what?" asked Trevor.

Sam shrugged. "I don't know. It's what they do on the telly."

"Before we do anything we need to decide if we're really going ahead with it." Ravi looked at each of his friends in turn. "And the question is, how do we decide? Do we have a silent vote using bits of paper? Or should we all raise our hands if we agree?"

"So now we're having a vote on how we're going to vote? Have I got that right?" asked Derek.

"Now you put it like that," said Ravi, "it does seem that way." He helped himself to a large slice of cake. "Anyway, what's it to be?"

"I prefer bits of paper," said Trevor. "That way nobody is influenced by anybody else."

"I agree." This from Ravi. "Derek? Sam?"

"Paper for me," said Derek. "Sam?"

"Me too," he said finally.

"Good!" Ravi smiled. "Now we've decided how to vote, we'll have a vote on the matter. Do you know, this takes me back to my banking days. Board meetings were just like this! Anyway. Derek, have you got some paper?"

Derek went into the kitchen and returned with a notepad and 4 pens and an elaborate, gaudily-iced lime and coconut special.

He tore off four sheets of paper and gave one to each of them along with a pen.

"Right," said Ravi. "It's a simple question. Do we get a stripper for Josh? Yes or no. Write one word on your paper, fold it and put it on the table."

"What if I change my mind half way through," asked Sam. He was clearly still havering.

"Think very carefully before you put pen to paper," Ravi told him sternly. "No spoiled ballot papers accepted."

"And don't forget," Derek reminded them, "it's all or none."

The room fell silent. The momentous nature of what they were about to do had hit them hard.

"Do I put my name on it?" Sam asked. He did want to make sure he got it absolutely right.

"No," replied Ravi patiently. "It's got to be anonymous."

Sam licked the end of his pen. He was ready.

The four widowers each wrote a single word on their ballot paper, carefully folded it several times then placed it on the coffee table. Nobody looked at one another.

"Shall I do the count?" Ravi asked seriously.

There was no dissent so Ravi collected all four papers and slowly, one by one, opened each out in full view of the other men.

"One yes," he said straightening the paper. "Two yesses."

The assembled group held their collective breath.

"Three yesses." Ravi swallowed noisily. The tension was unbearable.

Wiping his slightly sweating hands on his trousers Ravi slowly opened the fourth ballot paper and laid it flat on the table. Everyone leaned in further to see what it said.

"Four yesses," whispered Ravi. "Does anyone want a recount?"

The men looked at each other.

"Looks good to me," said Derek.

"Phew! Thank goodness that's over." Ravi was exhausted. "Well, gentlemen, that's the decision of us all. It's unanimous. We will get Josh a stripper for his birthday." He leaned back into his armchair.

"I think this calls for a small celebration," beamed Derek. He hadn't had this much fun in years. None of them had. "How about I make a fresh pot of coffee and we add a small tot of something to liven it up? What do you say?"

"Jolly good idea," said Trevor.

"But don't forget, gentlemen, that was the easy part," Ravi informed them. "Now we have to find our stripper and somehow I don't think that's going to be anywhere near as straightforward."

"Tomorrow's problem," Derek smiled at him. "Today we party!"

―――

Ravi drove home with a song in his heart. He hadn't felt this energised for a very long time. It felt just like the good old days when he was an under-manager of the illustrious Portsmouth Portfolio and Portmanteau Building Society on the High Street. He'd had authority then; he had it now. Position. Respect. What more could a man want? This stripper business clearly needed someone to bring all the strands together and he was just the man for the job. Who else in the group could do it? None of the others had the organisational skills he had. Ravi smiled as he turned the radio on and sang along to a medley of sixties songs. The unusually heavy traffic meant it took him almost an hour to get home but today he didn't mind. He was doing what he loved.

Home was out in the suburb of Wythering, a leafy expensive suburb west of the River Humble, where Ravi lived alone and had done since his wife, Geena, left him for a pimply youth from HR- Ravi had never had time for anyone from HR ever since.

Unbelievably, that had been only two months after they'd married and at the time it had been the talk of the office. True, Geena had been a lot younger than Ravi but then he'd had a lot to offer her; he was the youngest under-manager the PPPBS had ever had and he was earmarked for great things, he'd told her. Potential was his middle name. One day he would be THE manager of the Building Society with all the kudos and privilege that that bought. Geena, a clerical assistant in the mortgage department, had been tempted and finally succumbed and they'd tied the knot. Ravi had enjoyed planning the wedding, where his organisational skills had come into their own. He'd been in his element. Amongst his colleagues his penchant for lists was well known and was subject to a certain amount of derision. But Ravi didn't care and, if anyone had asked him, it was how he could explain his successful career in finance. With lists you knew where you were and the wedding was a case in point. He'd had a list for everything. From the caterers to the corsages, from the bubbly to the bridesmaids' dresses (all six of them), Ravi had arranged it all, crossing off item after item as each was sorted. The only aspect of the wedding he hadn't got involved with was Geena's dress. He'd felt it important for her to play some part in her own wedding so he'd left it up to her to arrange. And Geena, seeing that Ravi was spending an eye-watering amount of money on their special day, mostly without consulting her, chose the most expensive dress she could find. After all, you only got married once, didn't you? And if someone else was paying, well, all the better. And boy! Did she choose a dress! Made from antique ivory silk decorated with pearls and hand-made lace, it was a work of art and Geena looked stunning. But when she'd presented her fiancé with the bill Ravi had been stunned too. He had gulped in disbelief. Surely no dress could cost that much? But he was in love, he was sure he was, and having told her she could choose whatever dress she wanted, he'd had no choice but to bite his tongue and settle the account.

But there had been signs on their wedding day that all was not well. Geena had had far too much of the extraordinarily expensive champagne and insisted on telling anyone who would listen, and most people did (including an especially spotty young man from the office whom Ravi had invited), how she'd had almost no part to play in the most important day in her life. Not that she'd ever mentioned to Ravi that she'd wanted to be involved with the arrangements, but that wasn't the point. The fact of the matter was that he'd never asked her. Geena had finally passed out on the bed in the honeymoon suite of the hotel where the nuptials took place, still in her expensive, but now very crumpled and slightly grubby, wedding dress. Ravi was dismayed. This was not how it was meant to be.

After an awkward honeymoon in the Maldives, Ravi returned to being an under-manager at the Building Society and Geena continued to grumble. Even their new-build home in Wythering, with all of its state-of-the-art furniture and up-to-the-minute accessories (all chosen by Ravi), failed to impress her. She continued to complain and the scrofulous HR stripling turned out to be a very good listener indeed. So much so that one day Ravi came home from work to find a note on the hall table telling him that she'd gone. No mention of where or with whom - it was only months later that Ravi found out she'd run off with the pipsqueak (his non-appearance in the office should have been a clue). For a few months after Geena had left him, Ravi hoped she would change her mind and come back to him. He would have forgiven her, he was fairly certain of that. But after several years, during which time he concentrated on paying off the exorbitant wedding costs, he finally realised that was never going to happen. There had been no contact from Geena, no request for a divorce, so Ravi got on with his life, ploughing himself into his work. He could have been a bitter man, he told himself. After all, he had every right to be. But having decided that was a waste of energy, he decided to forget Geena and move on. And for him, moving on meant a life of dedication to the Building Society. His ultimate goal was to become the manager of the Portsmouth branch and eventually, in due course, he succeeded. Having fulfilled his ambition, Ravi was a content, if desperately lonely, man.

It was several years after gaining his promotion that he heard the news that Geena and her young man had died in a shark attack somewhere in the Far East. Horrible as the news was Ravi had felt numb but nothing more. He had been jilted, if not actually on his wedding day then not long after. No, Ravi felt nothing for Geena. Not when she left him, not now.

It was not until the issue of the stripper arose that Ravi realised that since his retirement from the PPPBS, something had been missing in his life. Not the humdrum daily commute to the office or the cut and thrust of the banking business. Definitely not Geena. No. Something much better. Lists! Now he could see a reason to write lists. He could not have been happier.

"I'm calling this extraordinary meeting to order," said Ravi pompously, rapping on the table with his teaspoon. The chatter ceased. He smiled as he realised just how much he was enjoying himself and how easy it had been to fall into his old managerial ways. He looked at each of his co-conspirators. Unusually, today they were sitting round the table in Derek's dining room. Ravi had suggested this rather than the lounge because of the magnitude of the decisions they were about to make and he thought that a proper table and chairs would make for a more productive meeting.

"What's extraordinary about it?" Sam asked.

"Because this is an extra meeting," said Ravi, "over and above our Monday and Thursday sessions, to decide how we proceed with Josh's stripper. And he doesn't know about this meeting. Remember, this will be a surprise for him."

"And for the rest of us too, I suspect!" Trevor added.

"Will we have to have more of these extra meetings?" asked Sam, praying fervently that they would. Any chance to get out of his house for a few hours.

"Quite likely," said Ravi, nodding his head vigorously. "There's a lot to sort out. There'll be things to do even when we've found our stripper."

"Like what?" asked Derek.

"Well, I think we would have to interview her. See what she's like."

"Why would we do that?" asked Derek. "I mean, she'll be providing a service and charging for it. Why do we need to interview her?"

"To make sure she's the right one," explained Ravi.

Derek and Trevor looked at him. The right one? More likely she was going to be the only one.

"Would we all interview her, do you think? Or just one of us?" asked Sam. "I don't think I've ever spoken to a stripper before. I'm not sure I'd know what to say. What would any of us say?"

"I think we'd best concentrate on finding her first then we'll decide what happens after that." Ravi was in full control.

"How do we go about finding her, then?" asked Trevor. He still yearned for red phone boxes and couldn't imagine any other way being as successful.

"I think," said Ravi, brandishing his pen, "the first thing to do is make a list." The man was ecstatic. A list! What more could he want? "Now, are you happy for me to write a list or should we appoint a secretary to do it?" He was trying hard to be as democratic and inclusive as he could, just like a true manager. The last thing he wanted to do was upset any of his colleagues or leave them feeling left out. Hang on a minute! He stopped himself. Colleagues? Dear oh dear! This was worrying. They weren't colleagues. They were his friends. Ravi realised he needed to rein himself in or he would be in real danger of upsetting them all.

"If we need a secretary," asked Sam, "do we have to go about finding one the same way we do as for the stripper? Go to the library and such? Look online?"

"No," said Ravi, "one of you could be the secretary or I could do it. Someone only has to take notes."

"It doesn't have to be a lady then?"

"No, Sam. It doesn't. As long as you can write that's the only qualification you need."

"I'm happy for you to do it," Trevor said.

"Well, if you're all agreed," (they were), "let's carry on." Ravi, thrilled at their unanimous decision to let him be the secretary as well as the chairman of all these wonderful meetings, straightened his notepad (bought especially for the purpose) and wrote;

    1. Find a Stripper.
    2. Interview Her.
    3. Arrange Birthday Surprise.

His list of things to do may have been a small one but he looked at it proudly before reading it out to the assembled group.

"Is that it then? asked Sam.

"That's the plan. Now all we need to do is identify how we're going to find a stripper and who's going to do the searching."

"Can we have a name?"

"What do you mean, Sam? A name for what?"

"This." Sam's gesticulation encompassed the entire table and its occupants.

"What had you in mind?" asked Derek.

Sam shrugged. "I don't know. Something like The Hunt for Red October. Then we can talk about it in front of Josh and he won't have the foggiest what we're going on about."

"I like that," Trevor said. "Like a codeword. Good idea Sam! You're full of them. What shall we call it?"

No-one spoke for a while. Ravi wasn't sure it was that good an idea but everyone else seemed to like the suggestion.

"I know!" Derek thumped the table. "How about Find the Lady?"

"Isn't that a card game?" asked Trevor.

"I do believe it is. But it could also be the name for our mission. And," he added, "it's got the advantage, as Sam said, that we can talk about it in front of Josh and he won't have the faintest idea what we're going on about."

"Find the Lady, I like it," said Sam.

"Me too," agreed Trevor. "It makes our stripper sound more human. More classy."

"I like that idea," Sam agreed. "I think it's important for us to remember that there's a lady at the heart of this. "Should we vote on it?"

"I think you'll find that as chairman, that's my decision," Ravi admonished him. Oh bugger! He'd done it again! "Sorry. I keep getting carried away. Old habits die hard. Inexcusable!" He looked sheepish. "I think it's a brilliant idea. Well done, Derek. All those in favour, say Aye."

Four Ayes later and their plan for Josh's birthday surprise had a title and a codeword; Find the Lady. In large bold capitals Ravi wrote it at the top of his list. FIND THE LADY. He nodded. A fine list indeed.

The second extraordinary meeting took place one week later. Once again, it took place without Josh who, despite the difficulty the four were having in keeping the matter secret, still knew nothing about what was being arranged on his behalf. Once again they were sitting round the table. On this occasion Derek had bought a seriously over-decorated chocolate sponge and, for a change, some small hand-baked oatmeal cookies.

"Now we have a plan and a codeword, I took the liberty of adding some stuff to our list. Things we need to do like allocating resources. Although I suppose you could argue that this is more of an agenda now, rather than a list. What do you think?" This could only have come from Ravi.

"Aren't you taking this a bit far?" asked Trevor, "What with your meetings and agendas? After all, we're only a group of blokes trying to arrange a stripper for a party. You're making it sound as if we're planning a take-over of the Farlington and Fratton Building Society!"

"It's important we get it right," insisted Ravi. "We can't leave anything to chance."

"But do we really need all this stuff? Agendas and resources?"

Trevor looked at Derek for support but the man merely shrugged his shoulders.

"Would you rather I didn't do it?" Ravi asked, his bottom lip quivering. "Someone else can take over if you prefer." It was the last thing he wanted.

Trevor shook his head. He never knew Ravi could be so sensitive. "No. I think you're the best man for the job."

Ravi breathed a sigh of relief.

"What resources are you talking about anyway?" asked Sam.

"Human resources," explained Ravi. No-one was any the wiser.

"And where do we get those?"

"It's us, Sam, We're the human resources."

"And we need allocating?" asked Trevor. He resented the way Ravi had taken control of things but he didn't want to upset the man; they went back a long way. But that still didn't stop him showing his irritation at the way things were being handled. Especially all this management-babble.

"Exactly! We need to task each of us with a specific task. Who's going to do what."

"And who's going to do that?" asked Derek, already knowing the answer. "Allocate us?"

"And how are we going to pay for this. The stripper, I mean?" asked Sam quietly.

It was the first time anyone had raised the question of how they would actually go about paying the lady and Ravi was furious with himself for having forgotten such a crucial part of the whole business. Trust it to be Sam who raised the matter.

"Good point Sam," acknowledged Trevor.

Everyone knew that out of all of them, it was Sam who could least afford to pay for anything that didn't constitute food or a bill.

"I think we should find out how much it will cost first before we decide how we pay for it," suggested Ravi.

But Sam was not going to let it go. "Don't you think it should be the other way round? Decide how we're going to pay for her before we find out how much it is? After all, we may not be able to afford it. Her."

More and more Sam was regretting he'd ever suggested they get a stripper. Perhaps Josh would be happy with a small cake from the bakery for his birthday instead. After all, he didn't know about the stripper so he wouldn't know what he was missing.

"I actually agree with Ravi," said Trevor. "Until we find our lady we don't know how much she's going to charge. And maybe, whatever it is, we could knock her down a bit."

"What!" shrieked Sam outraged. "Hit her?"

"No! That's not what Trevor meant at all," explained Derek. "He meant knock down the price. Barter with her."

Sam looked sheepish. Ravi decided he needed to move things along.

"If we're in agreement then, we'll find our stripper first then see how much she charges. After that, we'll take it from there. Happy?"

They were as happy as they could be, which was not saying much, especially in Sam's case. Ravi waved his newly-named agenda at them. "See," he said, "under Resources I've put Human and Finances." He was sure this would placate them. "Now remind me, when is Josh's birthday?"

"Two weeks tomorrow," Sam replied.

"That doesn't leave us much time. We need to get on with things. I propose we make a new list, to include all the places one might find our stripper. Then we'll divvy up who goes where to look for her. Agreed?"

Did they have any choice? Ravi produced a piece of paper from his pocket which he unfolded carefully.

"Right." He started writing. "Although I've started this list already I'm ready for any suggestions. I'd noted phone boxes down but drew a line through that one as they don't exist any more."

"Well done you," muttered Trevor sarcastically.

"And I've got the library, newsagent's and corner shops. Anywhere else?"

"Brothels?" suggested Trevor.

The three others looked at him aghast.

"Well we are looking for a stripper," he said defensively. "She might work in one. Or someone who works there might know where we could find one. After all, Portsmouth was a port, wasn't it? Still is. With a fine tradition of brothels, I expect."

"I don't think we want to go there, in any sense of the word," said Ravi, not liking the way the conversation was going.

"No, we don't." Sam was emphatic.

"What about strip joints then?" asked Derek. "That would seem the next logical place."

"I don't like that idea either," said Sam.

"What about a pub?" suggested Ravi. "Does your pub ever have strippers, Sam?"

"Oh no! It's not that sort of place."

"I know!" Derek slapped the table. "Barber's! 'Something for the weekend, sir?' Remember that? I bet they'd know where we could find our stripper."

There was no dissent so Ravi added it to his list. He read them out; library, newsagent's, corner shops, pub and barber's.

"What do you think, gentlemen? There's five places on the list and four of us."

"I think you can forget the library," suggested Trevor. "I wouldn't want to research something like this in public. Who knows where that would land you! And, to be honest, if you can use a computer you'd do it online anyway. So instead of 'library' I think you should put 'online'."

"That still leaves five." Ravi was showing that his mathematical prowess had not yet abandoned him.

"I think you should combine the newsagent's and corner shops. Aren't they one and the same thing these days?" suggested Trevor.

"Good point. So that makes it four possible locations and four of us. Couldn't be simpler! And now all we have to decide is who goes where to Find the Lady."

"Should we draw straws?" Sam asked.

"Still not relevant," Ravi pointed out. "Right men. Any volunteers?"

The men sat quietly whilst Derek cut more slices of cake. "I'll take the newsagent's and corner shops," he offered.

Ravi made a note.

"Sam can't do the online stuff so why don't you take that, Ravi?" suggested Trevor. "After all, you must have used computers with your job and when you had to chair all those meetings."

Was that a dig? wondered Ravi. He chose to ignore it.

"I'm absolutely fine with computers so I'll take the online search." He added his name to the list.

"Well seeing as I'm bald as a coot, I don't think I should do the barbers. Asking about a stripper is the sort of thing you'd drop into conversation while you're having your hair cut." Trevor patted the top of this head. "Nothing to cut here! I'll do pubs. Which leaves you, Sam, with barber's. Are you okay with that?"

Sam nodded quietly. He was so out of his depth but felt he had no choice; all this was because of his suggestion.

"Well, that's settled then," declared Ravi. "The sooner we start the better. Let operation Find the Lady commence!"

───

With less than two weeks to Josh's birthday time was of the essence, Ravi told them. He brought the meeting to a close making sure that each man was absolutely clear as to what he had to do and how to go about it. He stuffed his papers into his briefcase (resurrected especially for this occasion) and wishing his friends the best of luck in their search, he hurried out to his car. Ravi was going to strike while the iron was hot. He raced home to Wythering, exceeding the speed limit on several occasions, a first for him. He kicked the front door closed behind him and headed straight to his study to turn the computer on. Rubbing his hands together excitedly he could not remember the last time he was this excited. Was it when he was in the throes of organising his wedding? Or was it the day he finally made it to Manager of the PPPBS? He rolled the words round slowly. Those were his golden days. Unforgettable. Now this was going to be the same!

Ravi, despite his claimed prowess on computers, spent several tedious hours looking at websites and ads for paint strippers, furniture and wood strippers and page after page of DIY tools for the handyman who wished to do his own stripping. He knew he was looking at the wrong websites but somehow he couldn't quite bring himself to take the plunge. Finally plucking up courage he entered the world of strippers. It was not an understatement to say that Ravi had led a fairly sheltered life and he was disconcerted and saddened by what he saw. He realised that Kissograms came in all shapes and sizes, none of them pretty. And as for strippers themselves, he could only look at a couple of sites before he turned the computer off in disgust. The things people were offering was beyond his comprehension. Perhaps he'd try again tomorrow.

Derek was more than happy to trawl the one newsagent and the two corner shops in his locale. He was well known in Flotsome, having lived there all his life. Having started out as a quietly ambitious apprentice baker, he was able, after a few years, to set up his own small bakery and its location, close to a newly-opened railway station, meant it had flourished. He'd married, and buried, a local girl, Tessa, and raised two fine sons, one of whom now lived in Dubai and the other in Glasgow. After his wife had died, suddenly and unexpectedly, Derek sold his bakery for a not inconsiderable sum. He'd considered moving away - his sons had long since gone and he rarely heard from them let alone saw them - wondering if there was anything to keep him there. But Flotsome had always been his home and he couldn't imagine living anywhere else. So he bought a large impressive house close to the High Street and lived a comfortable, if somewhat lonely, retirement.

Yes, Derek was well known locally and, considering himself to be the proverbial pillar, he knew that any attempts to locate a stripper by visiting the local newsagent's and corner shops would be met with quiet respect but, most of all, circumspection. He had no concerns about what he was going to do and had every confidence he could achieve what was being asked of him. A search of the windows of the three premises close to where he lived revealed an assortment of cards advertising anything from garage rentals to requests for homes for six week old kittens (that one was dated four months ago), cheap payday loans to a request for urgent bric-a-brac donations for a jumble sale to support a local owl sanctuary. But strippers? Not a mention. Derek decided to try the newsagent first. It was where he bought his Daily Telegraph and he had no doubt his request for information would be well received.

A bell above the door jangled as he entered and he was relieved to see he was the only customer in the shop. Rows of neat, well-stacked shelves were filled with the necessities of life; biscuits, nappies and crates of cheap lager. To one side of the front counter were shelves displaying confectionery and on the other side, open racks of newspapers and magazines. Derek's eyes were immediately drawn to the display on the top shelf. One particularly eye-catching brightly coloured publication stood out. 'Hottest Rods' it screamed out at him. Maybe the answer was within but a quick examination showed that this was for petrol-heads only.

Derek returned the magazine just as a woman appeared behind the counter.

"Oh hello, Mr Draper. I didn't hear you come in. Just your paper is it?"

Blast! Derek's relief at the fact that he was the only customer in the shop quickly disappeared once he saw that it was not Tom, the newsagent, but his wife.

He nodded, picked up a paper and proffered a handful of change.

"Actually, Mrs Lowry, I was rather hoping for a quiet word with your husband."

"Tom? Can't I help?"

Derek shook his head. "Is he around?"

"Tom! Tom," shouted Mrs Lowry. "Mr Draper would like a word."

Tom Lowry appeared from a door behind the counter. Derek stood staring at him until Mrs Lowry got the message and disappeared through the same door.

"What can I do for you Mr Draper?"

Derek leaned forward and cleared his throat. "I don't suppose you would happen to know where I can find a stripper?" he asked.

"A stripper?"

"Sshh,"hissed Derek. "It's not for me!"

"It never is!" said Tom "What do you want a stripper for anyway?"

"It's for a friend. A birthday present."

"Strange sort of birthday present if you ask me. And why would you think I would know where to find one?"

"I just thought you might be able to help, that's all."

"I'll have you know I'm a God-fearing man! No time for any of that sort of perversion! In all the years you've been coming here, Mr Draper, I would never have suspected that of you! Rita! Rita! We've got a pervert in here!"

Rita appeared immediately brandishing a frying pan above her head.

"Pervert!" she cried. "Out with you! We don't want the likes of you in this shop. Get out! Go! Go on!" She came round from behind the counter waving the frying pan dangerously."And you can get your paper somewhere else!"

Derek wasn't going to argue. He fled, the bell jangling as he slammed the shop door after him. He only stopped running, or rather limping quickly, when he was several blocks away. It took him a while to catch his breath. This is dreadful, he thought. My reputation will be in tatters. I'll never be able to hold my head up round here again. And now I'm going to have to go elsewhere for my paper. And I thought this was going to be fun. He turned towards home, a broken man.

Trevor didn't quite feel the need for the same alacrity as Ravi and Derek in his search for Josh's birthday present but then Trevor had never done anything quickly in his life. It wasn't that he was lazy but Trevor was skilled in the fine art of procrastination and he therefore saw no urgency in starting his search for the stripper. He had volunteered to make the necessary enquiries in local pubs and that he would do but very much in his own sweet time.

Trevor left Derek's and headed home. He was feeling pretty miffed with Ravi, irritated at the way the man had taken over the whole business of Josh's birthday present and his insistence on having meetings and agendas and lists. This wasn't what their get-togethers were about. But then, he admitted reluctantly, if Ravi hadn't taken on the role of Chief Organiser, he doubted whether any of the rest of them would have been as proactive.

Credit where it was due, he told himself, but the man could still be a major pain in the arse.

He and Ravi went back a long way. Nowhere near as long as he and Derek had known each other but it had been a good few years nevertheless. Trevor and Derek had met up in Havisham Junior School when they'd been placed next to each other on the very first day and they'd been the best of friends ever since. They went through secondary school together then, as Derek pursued his baking career and his love of Portsmouth FC, something his friend completely failed to understand, Trevor opted for a spell in the Army. It was the first time the friends had been parted and Trevor found it particularly difficult. After 3 months he called it a day and went back to Havisham. He got a job as a trainee mechanic in a local garage, something that suited him down to the ground. It wasn't that he was especially interested in cars, it was just that there was no great urgency in what he did - servicing engines, MOTs, re-sprays. He could take his time, telling himself that accuracy was more important than haste. And at the end of the day, whilst the wages weren't startling, he had enough to live on and he could always supplement his income by doing a bit of work for friends on the side.

Trevor was Derek's best man when he married Tessa but, inevitably, married life took over and Derek had less time for his friend. They still managed to meet up for a beer once a month or so, but even that changed when Derek's sons were born. If they saw each other twice a year they were lucky. Trevor understood, of course he did, but he felt the loss of his best friend. Things improved when he married Joanna, the receptionist at the garage where he worked. Marriage seemed the sensible thing to do - everybody else did it. Derek had followed suit and he seemed happy enough. His mother, with whom he still lived, had expected it of him and reminded him daily of her desire for grandchildren. She herself, widowed after only three months, had had only one child, Trevor, and she desperately wanted to see him happily married with children of his own for her to enjoy. So Trevor obliged his mother and Joanna was an easy option. Derek reciprocated as best man and Trevor thought he would be happy. But he wasn't. The problem was that Trevor was, and always had been, in love with Derek.

It took Trevor years to realise where his heart lay. His marriage to Joanna could only be described as plodding. It was no great love affair on his part although initially she worshipped the ground he walked on. Most of the time he felt the relationship was a sham and that he was merely going through the motions. It was only when Trevor thought of Derek that he knew what love really meant. But he knew he could never have Derek and he was certain beyond a shadow of a doubt that his friend didn't know the feelings he had for him. Trevor was careful never to show any sign of affection to his friend that could be interpreted as other than just mates. What would he do if he knew? he wondered. Might his feelings be reciprocated? Trevor knew they weren't. So he tried not to think of Derek at all other than as his long-time pal, but his unfulfilled love for his best friend made him increasingly turn away from his own wife.

Trevor and Joanna lived with his mother in her home - on his mechanic's wages buying a place of their own was out of the question. They got along tolerably well but Trevor could always feel his mother's unspoken resentment when month after month, Joanna failed to get pregnant and produce the desired grandchild. Life went on, everyone growing more and more dissatisfied; Trevor with his unrequited love for Derek; Joanna, who couldn't understand her husband's increasing coldness towards her and Trevor's mum, with her unfulfilled need for her son's children. It couldn't go on and it didn't.

Matters came to a head at Tessa's funeral. Derek and Trevor had not spoken for well over 6 months and when Derek rang him to tell him the dreadful news about his wife, Trevor was heartbroken for him. Holding his best friend in his arms as the man sobbed uncontrollably, Trevor realised he could no longer live the lie. It was unfair to Joanna. It was unfair to him. That day he went home and told her that their marriage was over. He didn't explain why - he didn't need to. Joanna wasn't stupid. She knew things had not been right for a long time, almost since their wedding day. There was more sobbing but in her heart Joanna knew it was for the best. The following day she packed a suitcase and left. A few years later he heard that she'd died in a car accident. Trevor had been deeply saddened and full of remorse but he was gladdened by the thought that he'd given her her freedom.

After Tessa's funeral Trevor was insistent that he and Derek spend more time together, if only to help his best friend get over the loss of his wife. He was content merely to be in the presence of the man he loved. So once a week they'd meet up for a pint, a coffee or just a walk together round the harbour. It was there that they bumped into Sam one day.

It was Derek who noticed him first, a lonely figure sitting on a bench watching the seagulls bobbing on the water, his hands thrust deep in his jacket pockets. He pointed him out to Trevor.

"Looks sad, doesn't he?"

"There's a lot of it about," answered Trevor.

"What say we take him for a coffee?"

Trevor looked at Derek. Why not? Why not indeed.

"I'm just ringing round to see how you're all getting on," said Ravi. He was speaking to Derek.

Derek told him about the embarrassing incident in the newsagent's and how, following that, he didn't feel up to visiting any corner shops in search of a stripper. He'd been humiliated once and was not sure he could handle being mortified again.

"Oh dear," sympathised Ravi. "I can quite understand that. I've had a pretty grim time of it online. Some of the things I've seen would make your hair curl. I'm not sure I want to dig any deeper. What about Sam? And Trevor? How are they getting on?"

"I haven't spoken to Sam but when I saw Trevor yesterday he hadn't made a start."

"I'm not sure we're going to find our lady in time."

"Oh Trevor will get round to it soon enough. We've still got just over a week. You know he's not a man to be hurried."

"I know. But I do worry. It was such a good idea of Sam's but we're no further forward than when he first suggested it."

"Oh, I think we are. I've been thoroughly humiliated and can never hold my head up again round here and you've discovered hidden depths of depravity on the internet. I would call that progress," said Derek sarcastically.

Ravi nodded to himself.

"Do you think it's worth me ringing Trevor?" he asked.

"I wouldn't bother, to be honest. Give it a day or two."

"What about another meeting? Do you think that would chivvy people along?"

"Can't do any harm, I suppose."

"OK then. I'll set one up for Tuesday. Your place as usual?"

"Fine by me."

"See you then," Ravi put the phone down.

Ravi could not imagine how he could have survived without his twice-weekly meetings with his friends. Once he'd retired life had held little meaning for him. His life as the centre of the PPPBS had been his whole world and if he could have continued beyond his retirement date he would have done. But the Building Society had its rules and, come 60, he was expected to hang up his calculator and make way for fresh blood. These days you could stay on if you wanted to, he thought ruefully. If they insisted on letting you go today you could claim age discrimination. But back in the days when he'd done his 40 years there was no choice. He'd been presented with a carriage clock, a blatant reminder that his time was up. Ravi had had no idea how he would spend his retirement. What would he do each day? Travel perhaps? Start a new hobby? Learn to play the piano? But nothing had grabbed his attention and he could feel time slipping inexorably away. With no-one to share anything - time, meals, a joke - Ravi felt himself becoming gradually more isolated and more insular. It became an effort to talk to people even in the supermarket where he did his weekly shop. His days were endless. Empty. Lonely. That was until he'd met Derek. Serendipity is a wonderful thing.

One spring morning Ravi decided to go to a recently-opened supermarket, Pik and Chooz on the ring road. He was very much a creature of habit, shopping for his groceries in the same place week in week out, year in year out. But the store was new and the fact that the sun was shining for the first time in days persuaded him to give it a go. There had been a lot of coverage about it in the local paper and, whilst not in the habit of getting excited about such things, he certainly had time on his hands and, anyway, the car needed a run.

The place was heaving. Big mistake, he thought, as he drove round the car park for the third time looking for a space. Finally finding one, he parked carefully, grabbed a trolley and the glass doors opened wide, beckoning him in. It was overwhelming. Aisle after aisle of seemingly endless shelves stretched away into the distance. It took Ravi over an hour and a half to find what he wanted, battling through hordes of shoppers who acted as if they'd never seen food before, until he finally joined the end of a very long queue for the checkout. Never again, he muttered under his breath.

"What's that?" asked a man in front of him.

Ravi was startled. He didn't think he'd spoken out loud.

"I said 'Never again'. It's been hell!"

The man smiled at him.

"Awful, isn't it? I only came to have a look. First and last time." He appraised the groceries in Ravi's trolley; a dozen ready meals for one, 2 pints of milk, a small loaf of bread and four bottles of wine. "Looks like food for one," he laughed.

Ravi was indignant and was just about to give the man a piece of his mind when he saw him pointing to his own trolley and laughing. The contents weren't very different.

"Not easy, is it?"

Ravi knew what he meant. He smiled back tentatively.

"I'm Derek," said the man. "And I'm shopping for one too." He held out his hand. Ravi shook it.

The following week found Ravi at Derek's house for the first time, where he met the rest of the gang; Sam and Trevor. And that was what had saved him - meeting up with friends, real friends, twice a week for the past eight years. Yes, serendipity had a lot to answer for.

"After I spoke to Derek last week, I decided we'd better have an urgent meeting," Ravi informed Trevor. Once more they were sitting at Derek's dining table, the seriousness of the situation warranting upright chairs. "Derek told me what a disastrous time he'd had at the newsagent's and I wasn't having any more luck online. I thought we needed to catch up. It's less than a week now to Josh's birthday and unless we get a move on we're not going to get a stripper for him. And where's Sam? He knew we were having another meeting today. I thought he would have been here by now." He sounded cross.

"He rang me to say he'd be late," Derek told him. "Said something about meeting someone."

"I just hope it's something to do with Josh, that's all. How have you got on, Trevor? Any luck in the pubs?"

Trevor shook his head.

"I tried three pubs near where I live. At the first one the landlord threw me out. Not literally, but he told me to leave and that I wasn't welcome there again. The second wasn't much better. The landlord told me in no uncertain terms that strippers were exploited women who didn't have any choice in the matter. When I asked if he thought male strippers were exploited too he told me to bugger off. So I did! The third pub was run by a landlady. She was a bit more understanding when I explained why I wanted a stripper but she said she couldn't condone anything that devalued women. So that was me firmly put in my place."

"Hmm. I hope Sam has had better luck at the barber's," said Ravi, helping himself to a slice of fruit loaf.

At that moment the doorbell rang. Derek got up to answer it. It was Sam. He bounded into the dining room and sat at the table, grinning broadly.

"I've done it!" he announced proudly. "I have done it!"

"What? You've found our stripper?" asked Ravi.

Sam nodded vigorously.

"Better than that! I've not just found one stripper. I've found two!" The man was jubilant.

"How? I mean, where?" Trevor demanded. "In the barber's?"

"No. I didn't get that far. Derek, do you think I could have a cup of tea? I feel as if I've run from the bus stop and I'm parched."

Whilst Derek made a fresh pot of tea, Sam sat looking smug. Once he'd had a mouthful, he resumed his story.

"I never got to the barber's," he admitted.

"Where did you find her, then? Them, I mean. You said two. Not in a phone box?" asked Trevor laughing.

"Nope. In my local. The Articulate Angler. I popped in for a pint the other evening and these two ladies were sitting there. They had a look about them."

"What? Like a stripper?" asked Derek.

"No, not at all. They looked perfectly respectable. Classy even. I'd never seen them before. Anyway, the pub was quite busy and the only free table was next to them. So I sat down and listened in to their conversation. I know I shouldn't have done but I couldn't help myself. And it paid off. Guess what? Turned out they were both strippers, both desperately looking for work."

"What did you do?"

"I went up to them and said 'Ladies, I'm sorry for listening in to you chatting but I couldn't help hearing what you were saying. As it happens, I'm in need of someone like your good selves and I wonder if we might not be able to do each other a favour. At first they were a bit cagey and I can't say I blame them. Being approached by a complete stranger in a pub saying he wants a stripper. But I bought them each a large gin and tonic - do you know how much that cost me?"

"Never mind that," said Trevor. "Go on."

"Well, to cut a long story short, they are interested. One of them calls herself Little Bitty Buttocks and the other is Large Marge. That's not their real names by the way."

"Somehow I didn't think it would be," said Trevor.

"Large Marge and Little Bitty Buttocks? Is that the best you can do?" This was from Derek, annoyed that Sam had succeeded where he'd failed.

"They were perfectly nice ladies," replied Sam indignantly. "And, what's more, they're both up for it. So there you go. I've found us two ladies, interviewed them both and agreed a price." He sat back in his chair, proud of himself.

"Well done you!" said Ravi. "Bravo!"

"But we only need one," Trevor pointed out. "Which one do you think we should go for?"

"I like Large Marge. She had a lovely smile. I think she'd be great, but I've got both their phone numbers."

"Do you think we should vote on it?" asked Ravi hopefully.

"No! Absolutely not! I think we should go with Sam's recommendation," said Trevor. "Large Marge. It's got a nice ring to it."

"And don't you want to interview her? See for yourselves what she's like?"

"I don't think so," said Derek. "If you like her, that's good enough for me."

The others nodded their assent.

"And she's happy to come here," Sam told them. "You know. For the birthday. That's if you don't mind, Derek. I couldn't think where else we would hold it."

Derek looked alarmed. The choice of venue for Josh's surprise birthday party had never been discussed and never in a month of Sundays had Derek ever imagined his home being used as a what was basically going to be a strip joint. But thinking about it what was the alternative?

"Are you happy to make all the arrangements?" he asked Sam. "You seem to have done most of the running so far?"

Sam nodded.

"And what's the cost?" the money man wanted to know.

"Well, that's another good thing. Large Marge said she would do it for £100."

"That sounds very cheap to me," Derek pointed out. "What exactly does she do for that?"

Sam shrugged his shoulders. "I didn't ask. I presumed that being a stripper she would take her clothes off. What else would she do?"

"Having seen what I've seen on the internet," Ravi said, "you'd be surprised!"

"Well I think she's a lovely lady. They both were. So are we going to go for her? For Large Marge?"

"I think so," said Ravi. "All in agreement?" They were. "Right, Sam. Josh's birthday's on Thursday, right?"

Sam nodded.

"Looks like a date then! Go ahead and book the lady. See you all then!"

Thursday could not come quickly enough for the quartet of friends. It wasn't that they particularly wanted to see a stripper; they were more interested in seeing their new friend's face light up. Or at least that was what they hoped would happen.

Derek diverted all his pent-up energy into cleaning the house from top to bottom. He paid a lady to do this once a week for him but this was a special occasion. He wanted the place to look good for the lady. He also placed a large order at the bakery for a fresh cream strawberry gateau. No point doing things by halves. Sam spent the intervening days checking and double-checking that both Josh and Large Marge would turn up on the day.

"That's the third time you've rung me, Sam," laughed Large Marge. "I've told you I'll be there and I'm a woman of my word."

"Yes, I know you are and I'm sorry to bother you. But we so want this to go well. Our friend has had a really tough time and we all want to do something special for him."

"I think you're really sweet. All of you. I wish I had kind friends like you." Fortunately Large Marge couldn't see Sam blush.

"So you'll be there? You know the address?"

"Yes and yes! Now stop fretting!"

Ravi didn't know how to occupy himself. He felt saddened that his organisational skills had come to an end. What would he do now? He rang Trevor.

"I feel at a bit of a loose end, to tell you the truth," Ravi told him. "Not sure what to do with myself."

Trevor felt the same but wouldn't admit it. The only change he had made since the surprise was set in stone was to buy a new shirt and jacket which caused his mother to ask, somewhat hopefully, if he was going on a date. He wasn't.

"I really enjoyed making all the arrangements," Ravi told him.

Hang on a minute, thought Trevor. Didn't Sam do most of the running? All you did was hold a few meetings and make a list or two.

"If you're so keen on doing things like that, planning and such, why not volunteer your services?"

"What do you mean?"

"Well, with all your management skills which have been so much in evidence these last few weeks, why not put them to good use? I'm sure a charity would be delighted with lists and agendas."

Ravi scratched his head. Was Trevor having another dig at him or was he serious? Whatever, it was something to think about. He put the phone down with a lighter heart.

Finally the day arrived. The four men assembled at Derek's a good two hours before Large Marge was due. Derek checked the house was spic and span - it was - and the cake prominently displayed on the dining room table. Sam kept looking at his watch, sweating slightly. The doorbell rang.

Derek ushered a slim, dark-haired, attractive lady into the lounge. True, she was a lot older than they'd expected her to be but she still looked lovely. In fact, Large Marge was not what they'd expected at all. Sam was right. She was classy. Her make-up was minimal, her perfume subtle. Roses and jasmine, if I'm not mistaken, thought Derek. She was dressed in a beige mackintosh belted tightly at the waist. Looking at all four men in turn, she smiled at each of them.

"Will I do?" she asked them.

Trevor nodded. "I'll say! But your name. I thought you were going to be, you know, big!"

"Fat, you mean?"

Trevor nodded, embarrassed.

"I used to be," said the stripper. "That's why I'm called what I am. But now I'm not. Is that alright?"

"Of course it is," Ravi said. "But Sam, you didn't tell us the lady was so beautiful!"

"I told you she was classy though, didn't I?"

"And how right you were. Can I take your coat?" asked Derek.

"No, I'll keep it on if you don't mind. Got my working clothes on under here."

"So all we're waiting for is the birthday boy. Can I get you a cup of tea while you're waiting?"

"That would be lovely. Thank you."

Polite too, thought Ravi. She's got it all. He was smitten. They all were.

Josh rang the doorbell and whilst he waited for Derek to answer it, Trevor ushered Large Marge into the kitchen.

"I'll come and get you when we're ready. Do you need anything?"

She shook her head. "I'm good thanks." What a strange bunch, she thought. Odd but really friendly. So different from my usual audiences.

"Ready?" asked Trevor.

Large Marge took a deep breath, cinched her waistband tighter and sashayed in to the lounge accompanied by loud music pulsating from the phone in her coat pocket. She flounced up to the fireplace, wiggled her bottom and turned round, her hand on her belt. She stopped dead. Her jaw dropped.

"Josh!"

There on the sofa between two of the men sat her estranged husband.

"Margot!"

The men all looked at one another, except Josh who couldn't take his eyes off the woman.

"But," stammered Sam, "she's Large Marge! What are you talking about?"

"She's not Large Marge. She's Margot. That's my wife. Or was."

"But you said she was dead. That's what you told me."

"I never said that. I said she'd gone. She left me."

"I know what that feels like," said Ravi bitterly.

"You lied to me." Sam felt close to tears. All this had been his idea - from asking his friends to let Josh join their group in the first place, to arranging this ridiculous birthday surprise.

"You lied to all of us," said Derek.

"I didn't. I never said my wife had died," Josh repeated vehemently.

"Well, if you didn't lie, you certainly misrepresented yourself. You knew we were all widowers. You let us believe you were one too."

Sam tried hard to recall exactly what Josh had told him but couldn't.

"I didn't mean to. Honest! I just think it was a misunderstanding. And anyway, all I wanted was some friends."

The four men glared at him.

Meanwhile Large Marge, or Margot, stood there, shaking her head in disbelief. Here was her husband, the man she had left more years ago than she cared to remember. And she'd been just about to take her clothes off in front of him.

"You've lost weight," was all Josh could think to say to her.

She fled into the kitchen. Sam followed her.

"I'm so sorry," said Sam. "I had no idea."

"Of course you didn't. You couldn't have."

"Did you really leave him?"

Large Marge nodded. "Don't get me wrong. It was nothing he did. We'd known each other forever. At least that's what it seemed like. And then after a few years of marriage I just realised I wasn't cut out for it. We made a mistake, that's all."

"I really am sorry to bring you back together like this. What happens now?"

"I don't know. This is such a shock."

"Will you go back to him?"

"I don't think so. We weren't right for each other then. I can't see that we would be now."

"Is there anything I can do to help? You know, to make amends?"

Margot took his hand. "That's awfully sweet of you but I don't see how you can help."

They heard raised voices in the hall then the front door slammed. Margot picked up her handbag from the kitchen table. "I think it's best if I go too. You won't be too hard on him will you?"

"That'll have to be for all of us to decide. I expect Ravi's arranging a vote on it as we speak! Will you be alright?" Sam asked her.

She nodded. "I'll be fine. I'm a big girl."

"Not too big to have friends?"

She looked at him. "No. Not too big to have friends."

"Good. Because you've got four friends here you know. If you want us."

"Thank you Sam." She gave him a peck on the cheek. "You've got my number. Call me."

With that she was gone, leaving only a lingering scent of roses and jasmine in the air.

3
DEAD AND GORN

...

The Registry Office on the High Street was easy to miss unless you knew it was there, tucked as it was between a mobile phone shop and a vegan cafe. It used to be a tattoo parlour and many a wedding had been unceremoniously interrupted by someone wanting to show their undying love for a mother or dog in everlasting technicolour. The brass plaque on the wooden door was the only sign that this was a venue where lives could change, not necessarily for the better. Once through the door a steep flight of stairs led up to a nondescript room, the majestically named Wedding Suite, in which several dozen badly faded red velveteen chairs were arranged on either side of a central aisle, at the end of which was an ornate marble-topped table. Some of these chairs were now occupied; a dozen or so guests on either side were sitting in the first few rows nearest the front. Most had made some attempt to dress smartly – the men in suits which strained at the seams, (either because they'd outgrown them or because they'd been bought too tight in the first place), the women in gaudy tiered viscose dresses with attempts, some successful, at matching hats or fascinators. Each guest wore a corsage of a single yellow rose. Behind the table sat the Registrar, a portly woman of uncertain age whose pale green trouser suit matched the painted walls of the room perfectly. If it wasn't for her questionable black hair piled dangerously high and her bilious tangerine make-up you could miss her altogether. In front of her stood a man, late 20s, in a pale grey suit. He shuffled from foot to foot nervously, buttoning then unbuttoning his jacket, not sure what to do with his hands. Suddenly, without warning, Elvis boomed out through hidden speakers; "Wise men say, only fools rush in..." It wasn't until the end of the third verse that someone finally located the volume button. But it had served its purpose, waking up those who had started to doze in the warm afternoon sun but, more importantly, announcing the arrival of the bride-to-be.

Slowly, beatifically, a pretty young woman in a long, pale cream dress walked up the aisle, one hand clutching a bunch of yellow and white roses, the other resting lightly on the arm of a smart, much older grey-haired man dressed, very formally, in a full morning suit with yellow cummerbund. Elspeth, the bride, smiled broadly at the man waiting for her. He grinned back as he took her hand and gently kissed her fingertips. The Registrar smiled at them both.

"I welcome you all here today to share and rejoice in this important moment in the lives of Colin and Elspeth as the two become one."

Colin and Elspeth gazed into each other's eyes, hand in hand, as the woman droned on.

"I call upon these persons here present..."

They were oblivious to everything except each other.

"This place in which we are now met has been sanctioned in law..."

A door banged in the distance.

"If there is any person here present who knows of any lawful impediment to this marriage, then they should declare it now."

The Registrar looked round the room. Colin heard a commotion at the back of the room but the Registrar ignored it and none of the guests turned to see what was going on so he concentrated on the beautiful woman who was soon to be his wife. Finally, unable to ignore a voice raised in anger, Colin tore his gaze away from his beloved in order to see what was happening. What he saw made his heart stop. A tall, elegant woman, dressed in what could only be described as an orange marquee, was walking boldly towards him.

"I know of a lawful impediment," she said loudly. "He's still married to me!"

Colin crumpled to the floor.

The Registrar and Colin's best man, Kevin, helped him up off the floor and into a small room off to one side of the Wedding Suite, accompanied by a distraught, hyper-ventilating Elspeth. The room, no bigger than a large cupboard, served as an office for the Registrar – somewhere to hang a coat, sit for five minutes between ceremonies or, in the case of this particular Registrar, take a few fortifying sips from a small hip flask. With Colin sitting down and the others standing around him there was no room to move. He sipped gratefully at a bottle of water that the Registrar had produced but his face remained drained of colour.

"Didn't you see her?" he asked, looking at each of them in turn.

"Who?" asked Kevin.

"Jeanette!"

"Jeanette? What do you mean, Jeanette?"

"Jeanette. She's next door! In the other room."

"Are you alright, mate? You're not making sense." said Kevin. "Has this all been a bit much for you?"

"No!" Colin shook his head vehemently. "No, I'm telling you. She's trying to stop the wedding! How could you not see her?"

"Elspeth patted his hand. "Do you mean Jeanette? Your...?" She burst into tears.

"But you declared that you were a widower," said the Registrar sharply. "Is there something you're not telling me, young man?" Last year she'd prevented a sham marriage between two people who clearly didn't know each other – they couldn't even pronounce each other's names. That had resulted in a letter of commendation from her boss. Maybe now she was in line for another one.

"I am! I mean, I thought I was! But she's out there. Dressed in orange. Have a look if you don't believe me!"

Tentatively Kevin opened the door, silencing the concerned mutterings as every guest turned towards him. He looked round the Suite twice before closing the door.

"There's nobody there, mate," he said, shaking his head. "She's not there."

Colin stood up. "Are you sure?"

Kevin nodded. "You must have imagined it. You can't have seen her."

"But I did! Don't you believe me? What about you, Elspeth? Do you believe me?"

Elspeth blew loudly into a lace hankie the same colour as her dress. "I don't know," she whispered.

"But I saw her," repeated Colin. "And heard her," he added lamely. "She said I was still married to her. And that's why I couldn't get married today."

"I must agree with your friend here," said the Registrar. "I think the sense of the occasion has all been a bit much for you. You're stressed and imagining things."

"I am not imagining things. I saw her, I tell you. My deceased wife. She's there. Next door. Here. Let me have a look."

Roughly he pulled the door open. Worried faces looked at him expectantly. One or two of the guests tried to smile. He recognised them all. But there was no Jeanette.

"Listen, Colin. Elspeth. I'm sorry but we can't proceed with your wedding today. I have to start the next ceremony in five minutes. We'll have to postpone your nuptials until another time."

Elspeth let out a long sob.

"You'll have to re-arrange, I'm afraid. I'm sorry."

"But what about the reception? And the party?" asked Kevin.

"I suggest you go ahead with those. After all, you've paid for them. You may as well try and enjoy them."

"Enjoy them?" wailed Elspeth. "My day is ruined and you expect me to party?"

The Registrar patted her back. "I know this must be difficult..."

"You have no bloody idea," snarled Elspeth.

"Now, there's no need for language like that. These things happen."

"Really? Husbands see their dead wives at their weddings every day, do they?"

"Nor any need for sarcasm either." She started to usher them out. "I suggest you explain to your guests, Colin, that you're not feeling well and that you're going to have to postpone your wedding to Elspeth. I expect the thought of something to eat and drink will cheer most of them up."

Colin stared at her, totally bewildered. He was in no state to make a speech of any kind to anyone.

"Or I can do it for you, if you'd rather?"

He nodded. This wasn't making any sense at all. How come nobody else had seen Jeanette? What was going on? He needed a stiff drink. The sooner, and the larger, the better.

It was a sombre crowd which left the Registry Office and walked the few hundred yards to the Ardent Weasel, a small pub just behind the High Street, where the reception had been booked in the upstairs function room. As Colin and Elspeth entered the room in silence they were greeted warmly by the landlady.
"Congratulations to the young lovebirds! May I wish you every..." Then she saw their faces, Colin's clammy, his lips pursed, Elspeth's tear-stained, black mascara smudges highlighting her paleness. "Oh goodness, you look as if you've seen a ghost! Is everything alright?"
Colin glared at her, clenching his fists. Kevin, just behind the loving couple, grabbed the landlady by her elbow and steered her away. A quiet word from him in her ear resulted in her rushing off to tear cling film from plates of uninspiring finger food which had been laid out on several tables along one wall several hours earlier. Gradually the room began to fill up as the guests arrived and sat themselves at the various tables dotted around the room. Kevin guided Colin and Elspeth to a large table near the bar, along with Elspeth's father, now regretting the extortionate amount of money he'd paid to hire his ridiculous suit, and her mother, glaring venomously at her almost son-in-law. My God! How the ladies' weekly bridge club would laugh at her! The room was silent, everyone waiting for something to happen. Kevin stood next to the bar and coughed loudly.
"Ladies and gentlemen. As you are aware the wedding didn't quite go as planned and Colin and Elspeth are not yet husband and wife although they will be soon. Nothing to worry about but, as you all know, the best laid plans etc. Colin was taken a bit poorly at the Registry Office – probably the thought of marrying

Elspeth!" He laughed but no-one else did. "Anyway, by the time he was feeling better the Registrar had run out of time and had to get on with marrying the next lot. So all it means is that the wedding has had to be postponed – but you'll all be invited back for the re-run, although you'll be pleased to hear you won't have to fork out for another wedding present! But in the meantime, the reception is paid for with lots of lovely food prepared by the landlady here," he nodded in her direction, "and the drinks are free. So fill yer boots, as they say, and let's enjoy the party!"

Nobody moved.

"And once you've all got a glass in your hand, we'll toast the... er... happy couple."

The happy couple looked anything but. Colin stared straight ahead, Elspeth looked down at her lap where she was carefully shredding her delicate lace hankie.

Gradually muted conversation started and slowly one or two people stood, then slowly approached the bar.

"That's right, folks," said Kevin. "We're not going to let a little thing like a failed marriage put us off our food, are we? Eh? Happens all the time. I mean! Look at me! I'm already on divorce number three. So come on. Let's enjoy ourselves and before you know, we'll be celebrating the marriage of Colin and Elspeth in style!"

Kevin turned to the barman and ordered himself a pint and two glasses of Prosecco, one each for Colin and Elspeth. Colin downed his in one, burping slightly as he set the glass down on the table.

"Sorry, love," he said to Elspeth, as he stood up, "Just need to go and splash a bit of water on my face."

He made his way across the room, acknowledging the nods and whispered condolences of the guests. The toilets were through a door and at the end of a long unlit passage. In the shadows someone was standing outside the Ladies, blocking his way to the Gents.

"Excuse me," said Colin as he tried to brush past.

"You're excused."

Colin stared then sank back against the wall. "What the fuck are you doing here?"

"Well, I like that! That's no way to speak to your wife."

"Wife? Wife? You're not my wife, Jeanette. Not any more. You died two years ago. Remember?" Did I really just say that? he asked himself.

"You didn't think of me once today, did you?" she said petulantly.

"It's my wedding day, in case you hadn't noticed."

"Oh, I had. And you chose our favourite song. I can never forgive you for that."

"Are you serious? I can't believe I'm having this conversation with you. You're dead! So how come I'm talking to you?"

"Alright Colin?" Elspeth's father walked past him, heading down the corridor. Colin stared after him.

"He can't see you, can he? Is it only me?"

"What do you think of my dress?" Jeanette asked him, picking up the hem and twirling round.

Colin nodded. "Not everyone can get away with orange, It really suits you."

She smiled sweetly at him. "Not too OTT?"

He shook his head. "No more so than anything else today."

"Not the way you thought it would turn out, is it?"

"That, Jeanette, without doubt, is the biggest understatement ever!"

He looked at her closely.

"I did see you at the Registry Office! I knew I wasn't seeing things. No-one else noticed anything. Why's that? What's going on? But how come I can see you and no-one else can? They all think I'm seeing things. And I am. I'm seeing you. But they're not."

"Colin, you're burbling."

"You're a ghost, aren't you?"

"That's one word for it."

"But ghosts don't exist. Look Jeanette, I don't understand any of this. You died two years ago. I went to your funeral. I scattered your ashes. So how come I'm talking to you now?"

Elspeth's father walked out of the Gents and stopped. He patted Colin on the shoulder.

"I can appreciate your need to be alone but my daughter in there needs you. And her mother's in a bit of a state too. Come on back in, man."

Colin nodded. "Be with you shortly." He turned to Jeanette who was still standing there.

"Go on. Go and rejoin your party. Don't mind me," she said, pouting.

He reached out and pinched her arm. Solid.

"Ouch! That hurt!"

"Are you really a ghost? I thought ghosts were, sort of, floaty. But you're not. How come?"

Jeanette smiled enigmatically and with a flounce walked into the Ladies.

It was clear that no-one had any appetite for a party of any description. The guests picked at the food and nobody, apart from Colin's Uncle Arthur, never one to pass up on unlimited free alcohol, made any serious inroads into the complimentary booze. Gradually, one by one or in couples, they made their way to Colin and Elspeth's table and, not knowing quite what to say, muttered words of apology that it hadn't turned out as planned and that they really should be heading home. Finally the room was empty except for the unhappy couple, Kevin, and the landlady who was viewing the leftover food and wondering how much she could charge for it in the bar tonight.

"I'm really sorry, Elspeth. This wasn't the way it was meant to be." He tried to take her hand but she snatched it away quickly.

"It's alright for you. You've been married before but I haven't and this was to be my special day and you've gone and spoilt it."

Colin would have liked to explain that technically it wasn't him that had spoilt the wedding but he didn't think Elspeth would understand if he blamed it all on his dead wife. He didn't understand it either.

"We'll get it right next time," he promised.

"If there is a next time!" She stood up.

"Now don't be like that, baby. I couldn't help what happened." Elspeth looked down at him. "No, of course, you couldn't. I'm sorry. It's just that you picked the right moment to come over all funny, didn't you?" She sighed. "If you don't mind I'm going to spend tonight at my mother's."

"But it's our wedding night!"

"Somehow, Colin, I'm not in the mood."

He nodded. Neither was he.

"See you tomorrow?"

She shrugged her shoulders. "We'll see." And, depositing the shreds of her hankie on the table, she left.

Kevin sat down next to Colin.

"Well that was a real bummer, wasn't it? Never seen you do that before. Are you sure you're alright?"

"I'm fine, thanks mate. A good night's sleep'll do me the power of good. I just need to get my head together."

"You got me worried there, all that shit about Jeanette. Where did that come from? It's been two years. Time to move on."

I thought I had, mused Colin, but clearly she hasn't.

"What do you want me to do with the wedding presents?" Kevin pointed to a small table in a corner where half a dozen gift-wrapped boxes were stacked. "Shall I bring them round tomorrow?"

Colin nodded. "Give it a day or two, if you will. I need some space."

"Sure. Shall I get you a taxi?"

Colin shook his head. "No thanks. I'm going to get me a bottle of whisky from the bar. After all, I've paid for it. Then I'm going to walk home. Clear my head. I'll see you soon. And Kevin, thanks for everything. It's not been a good day."

The house felt empty without Elspeth. At least it would have done had Jeanette not been sitting on the sofa in the lounge, a glass of white wine in her hand.

"Bloody hell, woman! Can't you leave me alone?"

"Nice to see you too!"

"What's going on, Jeanette? You're dead. Gone. So why are you here?"

"I've never gone away."

"What do you mean, you've never gone away?"

"I've been watching you all this time. It's just you've never seen me."

"Watching me? You mean here, in the house?"

"House. Work. At football. Tesco." Jeanette shrugged her shoulders.

"But if you've been watching me in the house, I mean, with Elspeth..."

"She's quite the squealer, isn't she?" laughed Jeanette.

Colin looked at her in disbelief.

"You always did have a mean streak."

"Now that's uncalled for, Colin."

"Well it's true. And today was just another example. You spoiled our wedding deliberately."

Jeanette hung her head.

"I'm sorry. It's just I didn't want to leave you. So I simply didn't go away, that's all."

"You had a choice?"

"It seems so."

"Well if you had a choice then could you have a choice now and choose to go away, like immediately, d'you think? Go back where you came from? I've moved on. Why can't you? Why can't you leave us alone to get on with our lives?" He took a large gulp of whisky.

"You shouldn't drink that. You know it gives you heartburn."

"Jeanette, you're a ghost. You can't tell me what I can and can't drink. You're not really here, are you?"

"I rather think I am, don't you?"

"Please. I'm begging you. Just go."

"You don't mean that, do you?"

"More than anything. I loved you. You were everything to me. But you died and I grieved. And now I need to get on with my life and marry Elspeth."

"Why are you marrying her?"

Colin was confused.

"Why am I marrying her? You told me to."

"Did not!"

"Did! You told me years ago that I should marry again."

"Yes but I didn't mean it!"

"Jeanette!"

"Well I didn't. That's what everybody says."

Colin sank back into the armchair and ran his hands through his hair.

"Nooo! This is not real!"

Jeanette got up and helped herself to another glass of wine from the fridge.

"And anyway if you are going to marry again, it shouldn't be to that prissy little madam. Honestly, the things I could tell you about her."

"Stop! Stop now! Get out! Go on! Out you go! That's my future wife you're talking about. And if you hadn't turned up today like you did, she'd be my wife now. I don't want to hear another word from you!" Colin grabbed Jeanette's hand and pulled her to her feet.

"I'm going. I'm going." She straightened her dress and drained her glass. "Nice drop of wine, this. Can you get some more in?"

Colin took a deep breath and closed his eyes. When he opened them, Jeanette was gone.

Colin staggered up the stairs, dropped his clothes on the bathroom floor and fell into bed. He'd hoped to fall asleep straight away but it was clear that was not going to happen. My God! What a day! And this was supposed to be his wedding night. He should have been celebrating it with the love of his life, but here he was, alone. Actually, perhaps it was a good thing Elspeth wasn't here as the thought of Jeanette spying on them made his skin crawl. Just what had she seen since Elspeth had moved in with him? And before? Not so much a guardian angel, more of a perv, if you asked him. Colin closed his eyes and tried to sleep but he kept going over and over what had happened today. He couldn't even start to understand what had occurred. Jeanette, his first wife, dead for more than two years, had appeared on his wedding day with the sole purpose, it seemed, of disrupting the whole affair. And she'd succeeded. But no-one else had seen or heard her. How was that possible? He didn't believe in ghosts – who did? This was the 21st century, after all. But today he had seen and spoken with, at some length, his wife who'd died unexpectedly at the age of 25 from a brain aneurysm. He remembered how one minute she'd been cheering him on from the sidelines at a local football match, the next, she'd collapsed. In the ambulance on the way to hospital, blue light flashing, he'd sat and held her hand as the paramedics did what they could. Don't die, he'd told her over and over. I love you so much. I love you too, she'd whispered, fear in her eyes. Jeanette didn't make it to the hospital.

"The irony was, I never even liked football."

Colin sat bolt upright. There she was, perched at the bottom of the bed, eating a packet of crisps she'd found in the cupboard.

"Never could eat these before. Too fattening."

Colin groaned. "I thought you'd gone. I'm trying to sleep."

"Nah! We both know that's not going to happen. Not tonight. Crisp?"

"What do you want from me, Jeanette?"

"I just want to see you happy."

"Then leave me alone. Please."

"You were thinking about me, weren't you?"

"Of course I was! How could I think about anything else! You come back to haunt me on my wedding day! What else am I going to think about? The price of potatoes?"

"Sarky!" She munched noisily. "What?"

"I'm trying to work out what you've got on." He turned on the bedside light.

"Like it?" Jeanette stood to reveal a bright pink silk sheath dress embossed with black cats with sequinned eyes.

"Weird. But I like the way you've done your hair."

Jeanette's head was covered in dozens of tiny jet black cornrows the ends of which had been dyed the same shade of pink as her dress.

"Cool huh?"

"How come you have all these new outrageous frocks? And the hairdos? Is that part of the being- dead scene?"

"Yeah! Isn't it brilliant? I can dress how I like. Eat what I like and not put on an ounce of weight. Drink what I like. I'm having a ball."

"What's it like? Being dead?"

Jeanette shrugged her shoulders.

"A bit like life, really, but with less background music."

Colin laughed.

"But you can still do things?"

"Pretty much."

"And do you see other ghosts?"

"Of course. I see old friends, family when I want to. It's really very social, you know."

"Animals too?"

Jeanette nodded.

"Do you see Benji?"

"All the time. He still won't walk to heel though. Do you want to see him?"

"Yes! No! No, I don't."

Seeing one ghost was bad enough, Colin decided. The last thing he wanted to see was the ghost of his old Labrador.

"Yes, being dead is okay." Then her smile disappeared. "But I do miss you, you know."

"I miss you too but I've got Elspeth now. Or I did have, until you intervened."

"You'll thank me one day."

Colin stared at her. What was she talking about?

"Look Jeanette. What would it take to make you go away? Money?"

"Money? Why would I need money? Don't be daft. I've got everything I need or want. Except you. I never wanted to leave here in the first place. I loved being your wife. I loved living with you. That's why I came back."

Colin lay back down. What was he going to do?

"Can I get in there with you?" she asked.

"Absolutely not! Don't even think about it!"

"I won't do anything, I promise."

"No! No! Go away and leave me be!"

"What are you going to do about Elspeth?"

"What do you mean?"

"Are you going to try and marry her again?"

"Is that a warning, Jeanette? It certainly sounds like one."

Jeanette shrugged her shoulders.

"It had better not be."

Jeanette examined her beautifully manicured pink nails.

"Look, if you really care for me and want me to be happy, leave me alone. You told me to marry again and that's what I'm trying to do."

"I really don't remember saying that."

"Oh your good old selective memory again! Like that time you couldn't remember ordering that designer handbag online? Or those little black ankle boots? I could go on! But I remember it perfectly, Jeanette. It was that weekend away in Margate. We stayed in that little hotel with the creaky bed. Remember now? We'd gone for a walk after dinner – I seem to remember alcohol was involved – and we both promised that should either of us die, it would not stop us loving each other but nor would it stop us remarrying if we found the right person. Now I've found the right person in Elspeth and I want to make her my wife. I'm sorry but that's how it is."

Jeanette sighed. "Do you really mean that?"

Colin nodded. "With all my heart."

"Okay."

"Okay? You mean it? You'll go away and let me live in peace? You won't bother me again?"

"I'll think about it."

"You need to do more than that, Jeanette."

She stood, smoothed the wrinkles out of her dress and brushed crisp crumbs off the duvet.

"I'll be off then."

"For good?"

"Dunno. Haven't decided yet."

Colin swore under his breath. He turned the bedside light off and buried his head in the pillow. Jeanette took the hint and left.

The first thing Colin did after he finally got up was to ring Elspeth.

"How are you doing?" he asked her.

"Okay."

"I couldn't sleep last night I was missing you so much." Not quite the truth but he didn't want her to know he'd spent half the night talking to his dead wife. He had no doubt she wouldn't believe him and he couldn't blame her for that, but at the same time, knowing Elspeth, she'd be jealous. "Are you going to come back home soon? It's lonely without you."

He was disconcerted when she didn't reply immediately. "Elspeth?"

"I'm still making my mind up."

"Why? What is there to think about? You still want to marry me, don't you?"

"I think so."

"You think so?"

"I mean, yes, I'm sure I do. But maybe not yet."

Bloody hell! So now he had two women on his hands who were considering their options. How much more complicated could it get? His dead wife wouldn't leave him alone and his future wife wouldn't come anywhere near him. He sighed deeply.

"Can I come over? We need to talk."

"I don't think so. My mother is furious with you. And Dad? He's thinking of sending you the bill for his suit. It wasn't cheap you know."

Colin could not believe what he was hearing.

"I didn't ask him to dress up like a bloody penguin! It was his decision not mine. And I'm already out of pocket for a marriage that didn't take place and a reception too. Perhaps he could show a bit of sympathy. Your mother too! If looks could kill..."

"You leave my parents out of this!" snapped Elspeth. Tears were not far away.

"I'm sorry, I'm sorry. It's just this has all been a bit of a shock, that's all."

"How do you think I feel? My wedding day and you let me down. It's all your fault."

Colin had to bite his tongue. "Look, I've said I'm sorry. I couldn't help fainting like that. It's never happened to me before."

"It's not the fact that you fainted. It's why you fainted."

"I don't understand. I just fainted, that's all. It happens to a lot of people, even on their wedding day."

"But all that talk about Jeanette. Your first wife. You said you saw her."

Colin knew he was on dangerous ground here.

"I thought I did." Best not mention last night's conversations. "But as Kevin said, I was probably just stressed."

"Are you going to see a doctor? Get checked out?"

"I don't think so." He heard her sharp intake of breath. He knew that sound. "Not unless you think I should?"

"I do, Colin. I really do. You may have some underlying condition it's best to know about. I think it would be a really good idea."

"If it'll make you happy, I'll go and see somebody."

"And if everything's normal, well then, I reckon we can go ahead with the wedding again."

Normal? There was nothing about this that was normal.

Colin spent the rest of the day in front of the tv watching football. Although there had been no plans for a honeymoon, money being tight, the newly-weds had planned to have a quiet few days at home together before returning to work. They had jointly decided that a honeymoon would have to wait since there were other more pressing demands on their limited finances. Shortly after Elspeth had moved in with Colin some three months ago, she'd hinted that his house really could do with a new kitchen, the one he had was so dated. And while they were at it, the bathroom could do with a re-vamp. And wouldn't it be wonderful if they could convert the second bedroom into a walk-in wardrobe for her?

What was it with women and clothes? he thought as United missed a penalty. He popped the top off another can of lager and drank deeply. Jeanette had loved her clothes. Her slim, toned body could make a bin liner look sexy and the bright colours she'd always chosen – and still was choosing, apparently – complimented her dark complexion perfectly. He took another deep drink. But she'd had so many dresses. And shoes. And Elspeth was just the same. Women, eh? Dead or alive, they still liked their frocks.

And what about Elspeth's suggestion that he see a doctor? There was nothing wrong with him, he knew that. Jeanette had come back, and the fact that he could see her and talk to her as if she was still alive? Well, that was nothing to do with his health. He didn't know quite what it was but seeing a doctor wasn't going to tell him anything he didn't know. A psychiatrist? No way! There was nothing wrong with his mind either. Jeanette was as real as the day was long – even if she had changed and was more pig-headed than ever. No. What he needed was a medium. Or maybe a clairvoyant? But no. Didn't they get in touch with the dead and pass on messages and stuff? Jeanette was doing that already. No, it was a psychic he needed. Someone who could tell him how to get rid of his first wife, in the nicest possible way. Or did he mean an exorcist? He'd Google both after injury time, see if there was anybody local who could help him out. Colin got another tin from the fridge.

Colin didn't have too much joy finding any help with his supernatural problem. He read up as much as he could online but most of it was mumbo jumbo to him. From the little he understood he realised that it wasn't a psychic he needed. No, it was definitely an exorcist that was called for but it seemed that they only dealt with evil and malevolent demons, evicting them from possessed people or places. Jeanette was neither evil nor malevolent. True, she could be a real minx at times and she'd always had a wicked sense of humour and liked to tease, but that hardly qualified her as a full scale baddie. Would an exorcist be bothered with someone who was just a bit naughty? And was it possible to evict someone from numerous locations? Or did you have to do them one by one? He thought of all the places he knew where she'd been – the Registry Office, his bedroom, the lounge. But what about all the other places she might have been during the time she said she'd been keeping an eye on him? Maybe you got a discount for multiple evictions. It was no use. He'd have to speak to someone and get the full low-down.

The little information that was on Google mentioned only religious exorcisms. If asked, Colin couldn't really have told you whether he believed in any higher being or indeed in anything at all. He could never see the point in going to church – it ate into football practice – but he thought there might just be something in this religious stuff. Best not rule it out completely, just in case. What he did know for certain, though, was that Jeanette had always been a confirmed atheist. He couldn't imagine that that had changed since she died. Although you never knew. Best not get anyone from the church involved in this – the last thing he wanted to do was annoy her. Surely there must be someone out there who could conduct a non-religious exorcism? One that could be conducted politely and sensitively? Somebody who could simply say to her, it's time to go, Jeanette, back where you came from. Leave Colin in peace. After all, it was only what he'd been trying to do since the Registry Office. God! Was that only the day before yesterday? He didn't want to frighten her or hurt her. It wasn't going to be like that movie. The one he'd seen when he was a kid for a dare. "The Exorcist". He and Kevin had lied about their ages to get into the cinema. Colin had never been so scared. It was the only time he'd ever held hands with another boy. No, something more genteel and empathetic was called for. But how? And who? How difficult could it be? He already knew the answer – very! Colin decided to go for a walk in search of inspiration.

As he walked along the towpath, past the rows of terraced houses being pulled down to make way for new council offices, he wondered about the people who'd once lived there. They were long gone, most of them dead and buried no doubt, but had any of them left ghosts behind? Did the builders have to hire exorcists to evict phantoms who refused to leave? Or maybe they had a brickie who had done a night course in exorcism to earn a bit of extra cash on the side. He'd have to ask Jeanette. She'd know the answer. Colin smiled at the thought. But seriously, would he be able to find someone, preferably local, who could help him out?

He doubted it. He hadn't seen anything online which offered him any answers. There probably wasn't much call for exorcists in Yorkshire, let alone his home town of Ducksford. Dejected, he turned round and headed back the way he'd come, toying with the idea of a quick pint in town before he headed home.

Colin wandered along the High Street, trying to decide which pub to go to. Not the Ardent Weasel for sure. It would be a long time before he could hold his head up in there again. Maybe the Road to Ruin? They served a good pint of Farrier's Armpit in there. As he waited to cross the road he noticed a shop he'd never seen before. Polish Supermarket and Booze Shop, the newly-painted sign announced, Spirits R Us! He stopped in his tracks. If this wasn't a sign, then nothing was! He crossed over and peered through the window. Row upon row of basic grocery items, magazines and newspapers and bottles and cans. A small counter at the back of the shop, unattended. Nothing otherworldly here. But down in the right hand corner of the window was a small notice board to which cards had been pinned. And there, among the adverts for English tuition, water divining, trumpet lessons, one card stood out. He stared, mouth open. No! Surely not! Somebody was having a laugh.

Issues with Spirits?
Does your past haunt you?
Let me lay your problems to rest.

Too good to be true? Maybe. But it had to be worth a go. There was a name and phone number. Colin wrote them down and hurried home, his pint of Farrier's Armpit forgotten.

The phone number he'd rung had been answered by a husky-voiced woman who gave her name as Magda. When she'd asked him what he wanted Colin was hard put to explain his problem over the phone.

"Ja, ja," the woman had said, over and over. "I understand. Then you must come round and we will talk." It sounded more like tok but Colin understood. She lived on the edge of Ducksford, near the ring road, and she just happened to be free the following day. So now he was on his way to meet the one person who might just be able to provide the answer to his problem.

Magda was not at all what he'd expected. Nor was her house when he finally found it. She lived in the middle of a new housing estate which was still under construction. It hadn't helped that not all the streets had yet been named, nor that her directions weren't as fulsome as they could have been. Eventually, however, Colin found the house – a modest two-bed, brick-built box surrounded by identical properties. The door was answered by an attractive young woman, tall, slender, with bleached blonde hair and dazzling blue eyes.

"Magda?"

"Come in! Come in!"

From the husky voice on the phone he'd been expecting someone much older.

"Thank you for agreeing to see me."

"It was nothink." She beckoned him in. "Tea?"

He followed her into the kitchen where a small table was already set with two freshly poured mugs of tea and a plate of custard creams. How did she know exactly when he would arrive?

"Sit."

He did as he was told.

"Now tell me everythink."

He did.

"Will you be able to help me?" he asked.

Magda nodded slowly.

"So you've done this before?"

"Many many times. I have almost 100% success rate."

"And once they're gone, the ghosts I mean, they're gone for good?"

"Oh yes. Gorn for good. Dead and gorn. And it's good you come to me so early. The lonker you leave it, the more difficult it is."

Lonker? Ah, he got it. Colin let out a sigh of relief.

"But you'll never lose your memories," Magda told him.

"That's fine. I wouldn't want to."

"Good. Now this Jeanette. What is she like?"

Colin smiled. "She was an amazing wife."

"Aw, thank you," said a voice he recognised all too well. "That's so sweet."

And there she was, standing in the doorway, a vision in lime green with hair to match. His heart sank.

"What do you think of this dress?"

"Nice."

"Nice? Is that the best you can do?"

"Looks to me like the sort of dress that Perry Mason would wear. Or do I mean Larry Grayson?"

"Not sure who either of those are. Friends of yours, Colin?"

"No, you know, the chap who makes the pots. Oh, never mind."

"Who are you talkink to? Jeanette?" asked Magda.

"Can't you see her?"

By this time Jeanette had sat down at the kitchen table opposite Colin and helped herself to a biscuit.

"No, but I can feel somethink. A presence. I know we are not alone."

"Is she for real?" asked Jeanette.

"Sshh!" Colin told her.

Jeanette zipped her lips with a smile.

"So she's here with us. That is good. Jeanette, I want you to listen to me."

"Do I have a choice?"

But Magda couldn't hear her.

"I want you to leave Colin alone. I want you to go back where you came from."

"And if I don't?"

"Don't be difficult!" hissed Colin. "Why are you being so bloody awkward?"

"I just don't think Elspeth is the right woman for you. I'm trying to save you from yourself."

"I don't need saving. I'm a big boy now, Jeanette. I want to make a new life for myself."

"But not with her. She's so wrong for you. You'll be miserable. Honest."

"What is she sayink?" Magda asked.

"I know things about Elspeth that you don't, Colin," continued Jeanette. "She's so shallow. I can see right though her."

"That's pretty good coming from a ghost!"

"Is she sayink that Elspeth is no good for you? That she won't make you happy?" asked Magda.

"How on earth did you know that if you can't hear her?"

Magda smiled. "It's what I would say."

"Bloody hell! Now the two of you are at it! Can you both please give me a break!"

"Jeanette has a point you know."

"Stop ganging up on me!" Colin stood up and paced round the small kitchen. He looked at them both, his arms folded, chewing his bottom lip in frustration.

"I mean it, Colin," said Jeanette. "It won't last. I've seen her type before."

"Magda, will you please do whatever you have to do to get rid of this woman? Ghost. Apparition. Whatever." He pointed to where Jeanette was sitting.

Magda directed herself at the empty chair.

"Please, Jeanette. I am askink you again. Time to cut these earthly ties and go."

"Is that all you're going to do?" demanded Colin. "Ask her to go? Haven't you got a chant or something? A magic potion to send her on her way?"

"Speaking of which," said Jeanette, "A cup of tea would be nice, if it's not too much bother."

"It is too much bother. And you don't have time anyway."

"Do I really have to go?" There was a catch in her voice as she turned to Colin. "It'll be like saying goodbye all over again."

"For me too," said Colin quickly. "But we have to move on."

"Oh you are harsh."

"What's she sayink?" demanded Magda. "Is she agreeink to go?"

Colin looked at his former wife and raised an eyebrow.

"If I must," replied Jeanette resignedly. "But you mark my words. Nothing good will come of it if you marry Elspeth. It's doomed from the start."

"Noted, thank you!"

"And remember you heard it here first."

Jeanette pushed her chair back, got up and walked over to Colin. She took a good long look at him as if remembering every detail then kissed him on the cheek.

"There's a change in the room," said Magda, whispering. "I can feel it. What's happenink?"

Colin took Jeanette's hand and kissed her fingertips.

"We're saying our goodbyes," he replied quietly.

"I'll give your love to Benji, shall I?" she asked.

"Please." There was a tear in his eye.

"Bye then."

"Goodbye Jeanette."

She kissed him again and then she was gone.

"Has she gorn?" asked Magda.

Colin nodded.

"How come you told her to go and she did? I've been telling her to go for days now and she completely ignored me. Why did she do what you asked?"

"Maybe it's the way I asked. I do have some powers. And if they work, who cares? Jeanette is gorn and you are free. You can do whatever you want now. You'll never see her again."

"In a way, that's quite sad."

"Now you bloody tell me!" Magda was not amused. "If you'd wanted her to stay you should have said!"

"I didn't. She couldn't stay. I'm moving on. With Elspeth. But like she said, it was as if we were saying our goodbyes all over again. It wasn't easy."

"I'm sure it wasn't. But you've got what you wanted."

"Yes, thank you." He pulled his wallet from his pocket. "How much do I owe you, Magda?"

"Call it a round tenner."

"That's all? You've got to be joking!"

"I'm not in this to make money."

Colin counted out five ten pound notes.

"Here. Please. Take it."

Magda took the money and smiled at him.

"Remember what she told you. Elspeth will not make you happy. She was right."

"You don't give up, do you?"

Magda smiled.

"I know things. And so does Jeanette. Maybe sometimes you should listen."

"Yeh well. I'm still grateful for what you did."

Magda accompanied him to his car.

"It's strange," he said, as he opened the car door. "I've never known a ghost before."

Magda smiled.

"Not many people have."

"But she was as solid and real as anyone I've ever met."

"Some ghosts are like that."

"She will be alright, won't she? Wherever she is?" Colin asked.

"She'll be absolutely fine. And so will you." She put her hand on his arm and squeezed. "And if I can do anything to help, you know where I am."

He started the engine and drove home.

The house seemed strangely empty, even emptier than when Elspeth had left him. There was something missing and he couldn't quite put a finger on it. It wasn't Jeanette, for sure. She shouldn't have been there in the first place so how could he be missing her? No, it had to be Elspeth. He'd give her a ring, see how she was doing. It was a good few minutes before she responded.

"Hello?"

"Hi Elspeth. It's me."

"Me who?"

She was kidding, right?

"Very funny! How are you doing?"

"Fine. I'm fine."

"Good. Listen! I've been to see someone. Like you said. About Jeanette. And I'm all sorted now. Everything's fine and we can start making plans again. You can come home and it'll be just like before."

There was silence on the other end of the phone.

"Elspeth. Did you hear what I said?"

"Yes," she replied softly. "I did."

"And?"

"Colin, there's something I need to tell you."

He felt his stomach heave.

"What?"

"It's not that I don't love you. I do. Honest. It's just things have changed."

"Changed? What do you mean?"

"I don't know how to say this..."

"Try!" Colin's mouth was dry. Whatever he was about to hear would not be good.

"I'm not coming home. I mean, back to you. I'm not going to marry you."

"What! Why not?"

Elspeth sniffed.

"I've found someone else."

Colin stared at the phone in his hand.

"But it was only three days ago we were going to get married! How can you find someone else in three days? I can't believe this."

"Please don't shout at me. I didn't mean for it to happen."

"For what to happen?"

"Oh Colin!"

"I'm coming over."

"No!" You can't!"

"Why not? You can't tell me this on the phone. I need to see you!"

"No Colin. You can't. It's over."

He slumped into an armchair, not believing what he was hearing.

"Just tell me everything," he told her.

Elspeth took a deep breath.

"I don't want to marry you any more. I've found someone else and I want to be with him."

Colin could not believe what he was hearing.

"Who is it?"

Silence.

"Elspeth, who is it? Tell me!"

"It's Kevin," she whispered.

"Kevin?"

"After the reception he called round to see if I was okay. He was very comforting."

"I bet he bloody was."

"Anyway, these last few days he's been there for me. And I've realised I want to be his wife. When his divorce comes through."

"I can't believe I'm hearing this!"

"Well it's true."

"So you're going to throw away everything we had? For someone you hardly know? Jeanette said you were shallow."

"Jeanette? What are you talking about? She never even met me!"

Colin laughed bitterly.

"She didn't have to. She knew."

"I don't know what you're talking about. And whoever you went to see for help, well, they clearly didn't do a good enough job!"

"Elspeth you have no idea how good a job they did!"

And he hung up.

Colin sat there in a daze. Kevin. His life-long friend and best man. How could he? And Elspeth? The love of his life? His wife-to-be? He smiled ruefully. Jeanette had been right all along. And Magda. Maybe it was just as well he and Elspeth hadn't tied the knot after all. Better find out what she was really like now rather than after they were married. But what a bitch! The pair of them! He took a deep breath. He'd grieved once. For Jeanette. He was damned certain he wasn't going to grieve again, not for a feckless, two-timing bimbo like Elspeth. My God! What a close call! That was the way to look at it. They deserved each other. And he deserved better. Just then the phone rang.

"Colin?" It was Magda. "I was just wonderink how you were doing?"

Coincidence? Or did she know?

"Elspeth has left me. For someone else." His voiced cracked. He could almost hear her nodding.

"I'm sorry. But not surprised. But how are you?"

"Oh, I'm fine."

"You don't sound it. Would you like to come over and talk about it?"

Colin smiled. "Yes, Magda, I'd like that very much."

4
SO

> X ✓x ✓ x X

...

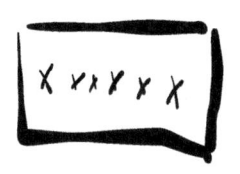

Lizzie stood in the bay window and watched her husband as he scraped out yet more moss from the cracks in the crazy-paving path that led from their front door gently down to the street. She rapped her knuckles on the glass. He stopped what he was doing and looked up.

"Five minutes," she mouthed, holding her hand up, her fingers splayed to reinforce the message.

He shook his head, not understanding. Lizzie disappeared from view and a moment later the front door opened.

"I said you've got five minutes. 'Til your programme starts."

John nodded and looked at his watch.

"Thanks Lizzie. Nearly forgot. I'll just put my tools away and I'll be in." He stood slowly, arching his back, groaning as the bones reluctantly re-aligned themselves. "God! I hate moss. No matter what I do it always comes back with a vengeance."

"I always said we should have had plain concrete."

John smiled and said nothing. His wife, he'd learned a long time ago, always knew best about everything.

"I've put the kettle on." She closed the door.

John picked up his tools and carried them round to the back of the house to the wooden shed, which, despite its tiny size, still took up half of the garden. Kicking off his gardening shoes at the kitchen door he carefully carried them indoors and placed them on an old newspaper Lizzie had put down next to the cat's water bowl. She watched him as he washed his hands gently but meticulously at the kitchen sink. You've grown old too, she thought sadly. Grey, like me. Grey and dull. When did we last have a laugh? A real laugh? Or do something different? She handed him a towel.

"You'll want to change, won't you?" Lizzie pointed to her husband's jeans. "You're covered in mud."

"It'll brush off."

Lizzie shrugged. "Do you want your tea in the lounge?"

"Yes please. Are you going to watch the programme with me?"

"You know I can't stand it. Nothing annoys me more. The way all the presenters start every sentence with 'so'. It drives me nuts. Haven't you noticed? They should call it So A Country Mile instead. It's everywhere now. I thought it was only young people doing it but it's everybody. Haven't you noticed?"

"Oh, it's not that bad."

"Oh yes it is, John. It's dreadful."

"Lizzie, why do we have this same conversation every week?"

She ignored him. "And the people they interview. They do exactly the same. So this. So that. It does my head in. It doesn't mean anything. It serves no purpose so why do they do it?"

"You just did it."

"Did what?"

"Said 'so'."

"But that was in context. And grammatically correct, I'll have you know. It follows on from what I was saying. But when they say it, those chinless, overpaid tv idiots, they don't use it properly. They say it without thinking. There's a big difference."

"Does it matter?" asked John wearily.

"I happen to think it does."

"I think you're over-egging it."

"I'm not," said Lizzie vehemently. "Come on! Just watch!"

John followed his wife into the lounge and sat as she turned the tv on, turning up the volume as the opening credits rolled.

"So welcome to another edition of A Country Mile," announced a clean-shaven, middle-aged man dressed in an expensive Barbour jacket, green moleskin trousers and a cloth cap. He spoke with a strong Geordie accent. "So on the programme this week we have Alan on his farm, counting the post-Brexit impact of the reduction in farming subsidies; Rakeem visits a care facility on the east coast for distressed llamas; and we'll be talking to samphire-pickers on the Cornish Riviera. But first, over to Louisa, who's walking the Pennine way with her Labrador, Crimson."

"See! See what I mean," said Lizzie emphatically, pointing at the tv.

"Oh, come on! Just go with the flow."

"Why should I have to? It's not natural. Listen! They do it all the time."

They both turned their attention back to the tv.

"So," said Louisa, "here we are in the Pennines." The camera panned to green, rolling hills and a cloudless blue sky. "And so this is Crimson, my dog and today we're going to be..."

"See? That's it! Everyone's doing it. I've had enough," said Lizzie standing, straightening her skirt. "I'll have my tea in the kitchen. Give me a shout when it's finished."

John shook his head and sighed deeply as his wife closed the lounge door behind her. God, he thought, when had she become so unhappy? Everything seemed to rile her these days. It's not just me that bugs her, he said to himself, although she does seem to hold me personally responsible for most of the world's problems.

It's anything you can think of. According to his wife, nothing was ever right. John tried to remember when exactly it was that Lizzie had changed. He recalled a lifetime ago that she was a cheery, bright woman, always smiling. Optimistic, upbeat, a loving wife and mother. Then suddenly all that had disappeared and been replaced by a scowling, complaining shrew. They used to have fun but nothing seemed to make Lizzie happy any more. When did she last laugh? John sighed again. Would she ever go back to the way she was? Could she? He still loved her - always would. But life would be so much easier if she learned to relax a little. Anyway, speaking of shrews, there was one on the screen. One of the Country Mile presenters, the one with the bright pink hair and matching beard, was holding a small, wriggling furry creature up to the camera.

"So, Barry, how do you tell a shrew from a vole?" he asked a small balding man standing next to him.

John forgot about Lizzie and concentrated on his programme.

Thursday was Seniors' Night in the Whispering Ferret. Two courses for £8. Cheap and the food wasn't bad either. Lizzie and John never missed it. Lizzie liked it because it was an opportunity for her to smarten herself up and put on a bit of lipstick. God knows, she didn't get much opportunity these days - they couldn't afford a social life. Not a proper one. The pub was as good as it gets. But she liked to make an effort now and then. Just because you had grey hair and a few wrinkles, she told herself, didn't mean you had to stop spending a bit of time on yourself. Not that John ever noticed. She couldn't remember the last time he'd paid her a compliment. Lizzie liked to look good but she knew she did it for herself. John, on the other hand, liked going to the pub because the food was so much better than anything he got at home. Not that he'd ever dare say that to his wife.

Having safely negotiated the slippery moss-choked path from their front door, they walked arm-in-arm down the street in enforced silence, having long ago realised that conversation was futile against the noise of the traffic. The pub was busy - it always was on a Thursday - but they found a table close to the kitchen door.

"Usual?" asked John as Lizzie took her coat off and sat down. She nodded to several other couples at nearby tables.

"Please." She sighed as she watched as her husband, dressed in his usual saggy-arsed jeans, T-shirt and cardigan, hobbled over to the bar. He'd long ago given up on any attempts to look smart, content to dress as the old man he'd become. Do I really look as old as he does? Lizzie asked herself. The thought depressed her. She got her compact mirror out of her handbag and rotating it slowly in increments, examined her face in sections. Hmm, she thought, not happy with what she saw. Thinning grey hair. Sallow skin. Dull, deep-set brown eyes. Even the smudge of lipstick she'd so carefully applied couldn't conceal the thin, mean-looking lips. She looked all of her sixty-eight years and more. Lizzie raised her chin, hoping her turkey neck would disappear completely. It didn't. Sighing, she put the mirror back in her bag.

A few minutes later John returned with a pint of bitter, a large glass of red wine, two sets of cutlery each rolled in a paper serviette, and a laminated menu tucked in his armpit.

"Here we go, love," he said.

As Lizzie studied the menu a teenage girl dressed in jeans and a white T-shirt with a grubby black apron tied around her waist approached their table. Her right eyebrow was pierced several times and she had a tattoo of a hummingbird on her wrist.

"Evening," she said. "So, the specials tonight are ham and leek pie and chips, mushroom stroganoff with rice or chips, or battered cod and chips. The soup's tomato."

Lizzie looked at her. "Pardon?"

"I said the specials are ham and leek pie..."

"Yes I heard all that," said Lizzie. "What did you say before that?"

The girl looked at her blankly. "I didn't say anything."

"Ouch!" Lizzie glared at her husband. "Did you just kick me?"

"Just order your food!" hissed John.

Quietly fuming, Lizzie turned to the waitress. "So I'll have the stroganoff. And the soup."

"So do you want rice or chips?"

"So I'll have rice," replied Lizzie pointedly.

The waitress wrote down the order.

"Same for me please," said John smiling at the young girl as she headed off to the kitchen. He turned back to his wife. "Can you not do that please?"

"Do what?"

"You know fine well, Lizzie. She's only doing her job."

"Yes, well, she's not doing it very well if you ask me."

"She's doing it absolutely fine. Stop being so bloody petty!"

Lizzie sat back in her chair, arms folded, lips pursed.

"Come on, girl. Don't spoil a pleasant evening out." John patted her hand. "Can we have a nice time for a change without you criticising everything? Try and relax."

"I could relax a lot more if people stopped saying 'so' all the time. You've no idea how much it bugs me!"

"Oh believe me, I do," replied John, downing half his pint in one swallow. "You can't seem to talk about anything else these days. Can't you leave it alone? Please. Just for tonight."

Lizzie sipped her wine. She sat for several minutes without speaking. "I suppose so," she said reluctantly. "But wouldn't it be nice if people didn't do it though? There's absolutely no need for it."

"Lizzie! Stop!"

The waitress appeared with two bowls which she placed in front of them.

"So, two soups."

Lizzie glared at her.

"And here's some bread for you. Enjoy!" A small basket of sliced white bread and 2 pats of butter were added to the feast.

"You didn't do it that time," said Lizzie.

"Do what?" asked the waitress.

"Nothing. Nothing at all. That's fine. Thank you," said John quickly.

The waitress shrugged. What were they on about? The old woman's clearly lost her marbles. She must have that thing that her gran had. What was it called? Dyspepsia? Something like that. Best leave them to it.

Lizzie curled her fists in frustration. "How can you not let it get to you, John?"

Her husband smiled. "Guess I'm a bit more relaxed about things than you are."

"You can say that again."

"Please don't start, Lizzie." Why did John always feel he was fighting a losing battle? At times he felt she could start a fight in an empty room.

"Start what?"

"Nothing. Just don't let it get to you, that's all I'm saying. It's not important. Honestly!"

Lizzie writhed in her chair. But it was. It was so very important. More important than anything else she could think of. She picked up her spoon and stirred her soup absent-mindedly. If she didn't feel the need to put the damned word at the beginning of every sentence then she could certainly see no reason why anyone else should.

"I'm going to have another crack at that moss," John announced as he washed the breakfast dishes the following morning.

"Can't we get someone to do it? I hate the thought of you down on your hands and knees, scraping away. It's not doing your arthritis any good. And anyway, I think it's going to rain."

"You could be right. I must admit it's not my favourite job. I don't mind a bit of gardening but I draw the line at moss. It's so futile. Can we afford to get a gardener, d'you think?"

"What? No! Of course not!"

"I don't mean full time, Lizzie. Just for a few hours. Help me get on top of the moss."

"Oh. Okay. I think we can probably manage that." Lizzie laughed bitterly. "Do you remember how we used to talk about our retirement plans? Sell the house, buy a smaller place and have lots of money? How we talked about spending our golden years on cruises and luxury holidays in the sun. Do all the things we could never afford to while we were young. At least, that was the idea. Look at us now!" Her face said it all.

John was crestfallen.

"It was a good idea at the time, love," he reminded her, "getting this bungalow. Our old house was way too big for us, especially after the kids left home. And what with my arthritis getting worse and you struggling with your sciatica. No, this place was ideal." He rubbed his swollen hands gently. "We just moved at the wrong time, that's all," he added quietly.

"We seemed to have done everything at the wrong time." Would she never let him forget?

"I know it was a mistake moving here, Lizzie. But it is what it is. We're here now and we've got to make the most of it. We can't afford to move again. You were happy when we first moved here. What's changed? Don't you like it here any more?" What could she say? She was unhappy. Desperately so. Everything seemed to have gone wrong at once. John had retired only to discover the small building contractor he'd worked for all those years was declared bankrupt and there was no money left for his pension. Lizzie had never really worked, choosing to be a stay-at-home mother whilst the children, Elkie and Dan, were growing up. When they'd left home, she'd had a couple of odd jobs but they were short-lived and not really what she wanted to do. So now, with only their two state pensions to live on, they'd had to economise. They absolutely had to downsize, John had argued. No question. After all, the kids had flown the nest and there were only the two of them now. They had still had a mortgage, albeit a small one, so they had to make some serious savings somewhere.

True, he agreed, it had been a lovely house, a large 3 bed semi on the edge of town and they had all been so happy there. Lizzie, especially, had loved the place, tucked away behind massive laurel hedges. With its rambling gardens and ancient trees, it had been her haven. But John was persuasive. Things had changed and it was time to move on. They needed somewhere smaller, easier to manage. And crucially, less expensive to run. So they'd downsized. And yes, the bungalow was smaller, a lot smaller, and easier to run. And it was on a bus route, with a bus stop only yards from their new home so they wouldn't have to rely on their ageing car. Well, it was on a bus route for the first 8 months until the service was ditched as being unviable. If only they hadn't rushed into things, she'd lamented at the time. We can wait. Just a few more months. After all, what was the hurry? But John was resolute. The sooner they moved, the sooner they could economise and have some money left over for the good things in life. But they'd sold at the wrong time, just as the housing market crashed, and had spent the entire proceeds of the sale on clearing their outstanding mortgage and buying this poky two-bed bungalow. There was nothing left over to pay for their dreams. If only they hadn't rushed into things became her mantra. The housing market would have bounced back, they'd have had more money in their pockets, a lot more, and they wouldn't have had to wonder if they could afford a gardener for a couple of hours' work. Didn't she like it here any more? She'd never liked it here in the first place.

"Aren't you happy here?" John asked her. He rinsed the plates and put them on the draining board. He turned to face her.

"Of course I am." Lizzie put her arms round her husband and squeezed tight. She hid her face in his shoulder so he wouldn't see her lie. "Although I would have preferred a bigger garden. And one with less moss! And not on such a busy road."

"Are you sure you're happy? I mean, we can't afford to move again but we could change some things round the place. A lick of paint here and there. Some more shrubs out the front."

But we can't change where it is, thought Lizzie. The main road with the incessant stream of cars. Or the north-facing lawn the size of a pocket handkerchief. Or the poky little rooms. Or the neighbours with their dreadful astro-turf lawn and their collection of Gothic garden gnomes.

"I'd love a new kitchen," she said wistfully.

John looked grim. "Now that we can't afford," he said despondently.

"I was just dreaming," sighed Lizzie.

"Maybe I should get a part-time job?" suggested John.

"Or maybe I should?"

John shook his head. "No. We can manage. We can afford a gardener for a few hours. Get rid of that moss and it'll lift the whole of the front garden. Just you wait and see."

"You're absolutely right, John. It'll make a world of difference." Lizzie was trying so hard to be positive.

"I just want you to be happy."

"I am," Lizzie reassured him. "I am happy, John."

He kissed her on the forehead. "Just as long as you are. I do love you, you know."

"Me too," she said. "It's just..."

"It's just what?"

"I don't know. Everything. Nothing."

"I've let you down, haven't I?"

Lizzie took his hands in hers. "No you haven't, John. I just get a bit fed up, that's all."

"Try not to, eh? Things will get better. I'm sure of it."

Lizzie smiled at her husband. "Me too. They have to, don't they?"

John couldn't think of a reply so he kissed her again and went out to his shed.

Lizzie sat at the kitchen table, her head in her hands. The bungalow wasn't the only thing that depressed her. It was everything. And she hated herself for letting it all get to her. She could remember happier days but they seemed so very long ago. When did she last enjoy herself? When did she last feel alive? She was starting to turn into someone she really didn't like, as if all her petty grievances were what made her tick. And she was taking it out on John. That was so unfair. But all too often she found herself being irritated by trivial, inconsequential stuff. Sure, the big things annoyed her. The traffic. Litter on the street. Rainy days. The constant scrimping and saving. But it was little things too. The lock on the bathroom door which never quite worked.

John's annoying habit of singing tunelessly in the shower. People who said 'so' at the beginning of every sentence. Lizzie had long since lost the ability to find joy in anything. Something needed to change. Or maybe she needed to change. But she didn't know how or where to start.

"You might want to watch A Country Mile tonight," John told his wife the following Wednesday as they sat in the kitchen eating lunch.

"I don't think so," replied Lizzie.

"Well, for one thing, it's live from near Cartsmell House, just down the road. You remember how you raved about their Christmas decorations when we visited last year."

Lizzie smiled at the memory. It had been a lovely day out, a rare treat for them both. They'd wandered the stately home's opulent public rooms which had been adorned with trees and tinsel and baubles and lights. Everywhere you looked was a riot of festive colour. Then they'd wandered in the gardens in the early afternoon sunshine, happy in each other's company, for what seemed like hours. There was so much space. So much greenery. "No moss here," John had commented. A lovely cup of tea and slice of cake in the cafe before they'd headed home ended a near-perfect day.

"And they're interviewing that actor chap you like," John went on. "The one who's got a huge farm on the outskirts of Bowledover. What's his name? Played the detective in that tv series. You know the one I mean."

Lizzie looked at him blankly. "I have no idea who you're talking about."

"Yes you do. Him. You know. With the hair!"

"Oh, for goodness' sake, John! The hair?"

John buttered his toast angrily. "God! I hate not being able to remember names. Do you think I'm losing my marbles?"

"No. I don't. You never could remember names in all the years I've known you!" She smiled at him. "Oh, you don't mean the detective with the limp, do you?"

"Yes! Him! that's the one!"

"Hardy. Hardy Sole!"

"Yes! Hardy Sole! How could I not remember that?"

"You know that's not his real name?"

"Thank you Lizzie. I rather guessed as much. But anyway, he's being interviewed about his rare breeds farm and how he does his bit for the environment. I thought you might want to watch it."

"Maybe I will this time."

"Today, in a special programme, we're coming to you live from close to Cartsmell House. The whole programme is devoted to what's going on in this area. We'll visit a creamery that makes all its own cheese from one single herd of Bewick cattle and flavours it with Swiss Chard; we'll talk to a man who, having spent some time in prison, is now recounting his life history in pottery; and we'll visit the only haunted bicycle repair shop in the country. But first, we are delighted to have a very special guest indeed, the actor and environmentally-friendly farmer, Hardy Sole of Inspector Solver fame. The actor is doing more than most for the environment and we are going to be visiting his farm on the edge of the Slattern Hills to examine his eco-credentials. It's going to be an exciting programme, I can guarantee you that! Without further ado, here's Hardy with our evergreen presenter, Carmen Veranda."

The camera zoomed in a bit too fast to the chisel-faced actor, revealing an alarming amount of nasal hair.

"Welcome Hardy or should I call you Detective Inspector Solver?" grinned Carmen, a buxom woman in her late fifties dressed in camouflage trousers and a matching jacket which was sufficiently unbuttoned to display a frighteningly large amount of cleavage for pre-watershed viewing.

"Ha ha!" laughed the tall, handsome, clean-shaven man with hair so intensely black it was almost blue. His moustache was an exact match. The man's teeth, displayed to full perfection, were so dazzling they could have been radioactive. "Hardy will do."

"Would you look at that hair!" whispered John. "Nobody has hair that colour. He dyes it you know. And those teeth! I wonder how much they cost!"

"Sshh," admonished Lizzie. They were sitting side-by-side on the sofa, mugs of tea and a plate of Jammy Dodgers on the table in front of them.

"So, Hardy," simpered Carmen, "tell us about your farm." She pursed her lips in what she evidently thought was a seductive manner.

"See!" hissed Lizzie. "They've started already. Why did she have to do that?"

John ignored her.

"So, Carmen, or can I call you Car for short?" Carmen nodded her head vigorously. "So I'm turning all my animal slurry from my cows" - the camera panned to a field full of sheep - "into pellets."

"That's amazing, Hardy," the presenter replied breathlessly. "When you say 'slurry' you mean…?"

"Yes I do. Cow droppings!"

"Wow! Amazing! And what are you going to do with these pellets?"

"To be honest, I'm not quite sure at the moment. So I'm very eco-aware as you know, I'll find a purpose for them at some stage."

"So that's absolutely fascinating," gushed Carmen. "Pellets. My! Who'd have thought it! And what else are you doing to save the planet?"

"Would you like to see what I'm doing with the hair I comb from my rare Bearded Bagshot goats?"

"More than anything," Carmen gushed again.

"Good. I think you'll find you're in for a real surprise. So come this way," said Hardy, setting off with a limp, "and watch where you walk."

The camera turned its attention to two pigs rolling in mud.

"So..."

"Stop it! Stop it!" cried Lizzie. "Enough, you stupid people!" She was on her feet, shouting and gesticulating at the television screen. Carmen stared directly into the camera, her mouth a gaping hole. She put her hand to her throat as if she was choking and tried to speak. Nothing came out. She grabbed Hardy's arm and made a rolling motion with her hand, trying to suggest that he say something. The actor opened his mouth but could only grunt. His eyes were wide in panic. Suddenly the screen went blank. John looked on in amazement as Lizzie sat down, clearly in shock. Neither of them spoke. After about thirty seconds a disembodied voice from the tv apologised for the technical problem and assured the viewers that normal service would be resumed as soon as possible. Meanwhile here was some music.

John looked at his wife. "What on earth happened? What did you do, Lizzie?" he asked her in awe. "What did you just do?"

⁂

John and Lizzie continued to sit staring at the blank screen.

"What do you mean, what did I do? I didn't do anything," she said, visibly shaken. She was trembling violently. "That wasn't me."

"Are you sure?"

"Of course I'm sure! How could me shouting at the tv make that happen? It's obviously some sort of technical problem as they said."

John turned to stare at his wife. "That was no technical problem. Neither of them could speak, Lizzie. It was you! You shouting at them because they kept saying 'so'. That's what did it!"

"That's nonsense. It's not possible. It's just not. Try another channel."

John turned over to ITV and, silently, they watched an advert for an organic wart remover.

"See," said Lizzie, "ITV's working. It's just BBC that's got a problem. Nothing to do with me at all."

"That's pre-recorded," John pointed out. "A Country Mile was live."

"I can't see that that makes any difference."

"It might do. And anyway, nobody in the ad said 'so'. Let's wait for an advert or a programme when they say 'so' all the time and see what happens."

They sat watching for a full five minutes before the adverts ended and a programme on exercise for dogs resumed.

"As I said earlier," said a bronzed, leotarded, heavily-bearded man clutching a chihuahua under his arm, "So, Pilates for Pooches is the name of the game. So, you and your hairy loved one - and I'm not talking about your wife, you cheeky things! - can double your fun. (His face would have broken into a smile had it not been firmly secured in place by an over-indulgence of Botox). Yes, you and your canine companion can exercise together. So a simple regime will bring you closer together and get you both in great shape. Follow my programme of stretches and bends or, even better, buy my new DVD available only in good supermarkets..."

"There we go! Now's you chance. Try it again!"

"I don't know what to do," wailed Lizzie.

"Stand up and shout at him. Before I do! Please! The sooner the better! The man is awful!"

Lizzie stood up and stared at the TV. "I don't know what to say."

"Do what you did before. Tell him to stop."

She put her hands on her hips. "Stop!" she shouted. No effect.

"Wave you hands at him. Point! Like you did last time."

She did as she was told. "Stop it! Stop it now!" Nothing. "See. I told you it was stupid."

John shook his head. "It has to be because it's pre-recorded. Let's try it with another live programme. I know. What about the news?"

Lizzie looked at her watch. "Too early."

"I'll go and put the kettle on," John stood. He turned the tv off.

Lizzie sat chewing her bottom lip, wringing her hands. At least the shaking had stopped. She hadn't really done that, had she? Made two people stop talking all because they annoyed her over one little word? It simply wasn't possible. There had to be another explanation. Okay. Maybe not a technical issue, John was probably right. But something had happened to cause the tv presenter and the actor on A Country Mile to lose the ability to speak. Completely. And it was awfully coincidental that it happened when she was shouting at the tv. She wondered how long their affliction would last? Minutes? Days? Until the next programme? Forever? The thought terrified her. What if it was her doing? What if she was capable of inflicting silence on someone who irritated her? Just by shouting at them? Scary. But at the same time, Lizzie felt a thrill of excitement. It had shut them up and they weren't annoying her any more. What else might she be able to do?

John handed her a mug of tea. "You're smiling," he said.

"Am I?" She shook her head. "I didn't mean to. This is not happening, right? I did not cause this to happen."

"Who knows? Maybe you did. We'll wait for the news and you can try it again."

"But if I did… If it was me… What other live programmes are there?"

"Weather forecasts. Those political debates. Sometimes there are ballets on live. Or operas."

"If I'm not mistaken, John, I can't see ballet dancers saying 'so' when they're in the middle of a pas de deux or whatever it is they're called. Although, come to think of it, opera singers might."

John laughed. He hadn't done that in a while. Lizzie smiled at him. "Roll on the late night news!"

"It's ten thirty and welcome to the late night news, whether you're in Aberystwyth or Azerbaijan, Zennor or Zimbabwe. Welcome. I'm Jilly Buttons and here are the headlines." A middle-aged woman, dressed in what looked like a surgical gown and with a surfeit of make-up and hair, smiled at the camera. "The UK's largest supermarket chain, Al Fresco, is cutting the price of fuel by two pence a litre. So unusually warm weather on the south coast has seen hordes flocking to the beaches. And there's been a further outbreak of war in the sub-Saharan region of Distopia with thousands made homeless and a famine forecast. So on tonight's programme..."

Lizzie stood. "That's twice she'd said 'so' when she didn't have to."

"Hang on a minute," said John, putting a restraining hand on her arm. "Let's see what happens."

She sat down.

Jilly read from the autocue in a flat, passionless voice, John and Lizzie hanging on her every word. Then suddenly the newsreader became animated. "And we have some breaking news just in for you." Jilly fiddled with her earpiece, a look of concern marring her perfect face. "So the popular tv programme, A Country Mile, which deals with all manner of country affairs, was unexpectedly taken off the air tonight as one of the presenters and a person she was interviewing appear to have suddenly lost the ability to speak."

John and Lizzie looked at each other. She reached for his hand. "I never thought it would make the news," she whispered.

"So it would appear that presenter, Carmen Veranda, suddenly found herself unable to talk. Unusually this was a live production of the award-winning programme. Unable to speak, Carmen gesticulated that Hardy Sole, the actor, whom she was interviewing, should continue but he, too, had lost his voice. So both have been taken to hospital for checks but the makers of the programme assure us there is no cause for alarm. So we'll bring you further news as it comes in."

"That's it!" cried Lizzie, standing up. "It's disgraceful! Stop it! Stop it now! War and famine and all she can talk about is complete nonentities who can't even speak good English! Enough I say!"

And it was. Jilly Buttons stopped smiling and tried to speak. But nothing came out of her mouth no matter how hard she tried to manoeuvre her lips. The best she could do was a croaking "Argh! Argh!" There was a look of sheer panic in her overly blue eyes. She clutched her throat as the screen went black.

"Bloody hell, Lizzie! You've just gone and done it again! What else can you do?"

"I don't believe that," gasped Lizzie. "I mean, what just happened?"
"You did it again!"
"It certainly seems so." She shook her head in disbelief. "But how?"
"I have no idea. Want to try it again?"

"I don't know. It's all a bit scary, to tell the truth." Lizzie absent-mindedly ate another biscuit. After a moment, she looked at John, a twinkle in her eye. "Go on then! What else is on?"

"Let's try the late weather on Channel 4. Although quite often they pre-record the forecasts from earlier in the day." He flicked through the channels until he found the right one. "This'll do. It's the local forecast."

"Tonight there will be another warm front heading up from the Sahara," announced an elderly man in a brown suit that had seen better days. "So the weather will be warmer than usual for this time of year." John looked at Lizzie questioningly but she shook her head.

"That's ok. He's using 'so' properly there."

"You know best," muttered John.

The weatherman continued. "Winds will be light but those living up on the moors shouldn't be surprised if they have the odd shower. So high tide tonight at Scareborough will be at 1220 and at 1230 at Farmborough Head. So don't forget tomorrow is the annual goat-cart race at Kirby Whisperton with all proceeds going to…."

Lizzie stood up quickly. "Stop!" she shouted. The weatherman looked alarmed. Lizzie looked at her husband. "What do I say next?" she demanded. "Do I have to say the same thing? I've said different things every time, haven't I?"

"I don't know," shouted John. "Say something! Anything! Quick! Before the forecast ends! Just see what happens!"

"Stop! Stop, you stupid man! I forbid you to say another word!"

The weather forecaster did as he was told, leaving the viewers never knowing who would benefit from the goat-cart race. The man had been rendered dumb.

"Bloody hell!" laughed John. "You've only gone and done it again. At this rate, there'll be nobody left on the telly!"

Lizzie sat down heavily. "I've done it! I've really done it, haven't I?"

"You sure have."

"But what does it mean?"

"I have no idea," replied John. "No idea at all."

"I still can't work out how it happened. It doesn't make any sense."

"Well, Mrs Braddon. We now have to take it up a level."

"What do you mean?"

"Well, on all three occasions tonight you made people on the tv lose the ability to speak. But only when the programmes were live. We need to see how it works in the real world."

"You mean…?"

"Yup. Tomorrow we hit the town!"

Lizzie didn't get a wink of sleep all night. She replayed the entire evening over and over in her head. How could she, a housewife, a mother, just an ordinary human being who'd never done anything remarkable ever, how could she conjure up these magic powers? Because that was what she was certain they were, to have this effect on people she didn't know. Would it work on people she did know? she wondered. John? Her children? The awful couple next door. She smiled at the thought. Frank and Filly showing off their latest purchase from the garden centre. "Here's Fred the fisherman," she imagined them saying. "So look at his miniature..." Oh yes! That would be such a result. To cut them both off mid-sentence. But where would it end? Eventually she gave up trying to sleep and went downstairs to make herself a cup of tea. It wasn't long before John joined her.

"Couldn't sleep?" he asked her. "Me neither."

"Do you think I could be prosecuted?" Lizzie asked him.

"For what? I can't see that you've committed any crime. I think you've done the world a favour!"

"Don't you think I've harmed these people?"

John pondered the idea. "I can't see how."

"ABH? I have inflicted harm on them. Do you think I need a lawyer?"

John laughed uproariously. "Harm? I don't think so. It's bodily harm and you haven't harmed their bodies at all, have you?"

"I rather think I have. I've deprived them of a major function."

"But they might get it back. We don't know, do we?"

"But what if they don't? What if they never speak again? Could I be sent to prison? What would Elkie and Dan say?" Lizzie found a tissue in the pocket of her dressing gown and blew her nose.

John patted her hand. "I think you're worrying unnecessarily, love. Let's see what happens in town today. And we'll keep an eye on the news."

"I really am worried, you know."

"I know. But nobody can prove it was you. And who knows, you may have other powers that you don't know about."

"Like what?"

"I don't know. Picking the winning lottery numbers. Or the winner of the 3.30 at Kimpton. Knowing exactly what the weather's going to do. Finding a cure for our moss problem!"

"God! Wouldn't that be brilliant! Winning the lottery, I mean. We could buy a new house. Move away from here. Give some money to the kids. Shall we get a ticket tomorrow?"

John looked sad. "You don't like it here, do you?"

"I never said that."

"You didn't have to. "

"All I'm saying, John, is that if we did win lots of money, if I do have special powers, then it gives us choices, doesn't it?"

He nodded. "I suppose so. But don't go building your hopes up. Now come back to bed."

John and Lizzie sat upstairs on the bus. They'd got up early since neither of them could go back to sleep. Despite a disturbed night for both of them, they were as excited as kids on Christmas morning. Nothing this momentous had ever happened to them before. After an early breakfast they'd had to cool their heels, waiting impatiently for the magic hour when their bus passes would kick in. Despite the nearest bus stop now being nearly half a mile away from their bungalow, John didn't like using the car, and despite their eagerness to get into Yorbridge and put Lizzie's new-found powers to the test, this morning was no exception. Taking the car was too expensive and city centre parking was extortionate. The bus was pretty full, mostly with seniors heading into town, but it was quiet apart from a teenager who was sitting half a dozen seats in front of them. His neck was black with tattoos and he sported a red baseball cap, the peak over his right ear. He was talking to someone very loudly on his phone. Unfortunately his conversation was shared by the entire upper deck.

"D'ya know what she fuckin' said to me? Me? Her fuckin' boyfriend? So she said I 'ad fuckin' bad bref."

"Bref?" John mouthed to Lizzie. She pointed at her mouth. "Ah!"

"Cow! Fuckin' cow! So she don't know nuffin! If she finks for one moment that I'm going to pay for her on Friday night. Well, I fuckin' ain't."

Lizzie looked across the aisle at a young girl who was trying to distract a toddler from the dreadful language by singing nursery rhymes. The girl looked up and grimaced. An elderly woman sitting behind her tutted noisily. Lizzie turned round to look at the other passengers. Several shook their heads. Others just looked away.

"Why don't you try it on him?" John asked his wife.

"Really?"

"Why not? What have you got to lose? His language is vile and that poor girl, trying to stop the little one listening. Go on! Give it a go! You'd be doing everyone a favour."

"I can't just go and tell him to stop. What if he turns nasty? Tries to hit me or something?"

"Try thought waves," suggested John. "You know, telepathic thought transference thing. See if that works. And if it doesn't, whisper it."

Lizzie looked doubtful. But somebody had to do something. Here goes, she thought. Her face assumed what she believed was a determined look. She screwed her eyes up tight and furrowed her brows. Focus, she told herself. Concentrate on making him stop. She screwed her eyes even tighter until her head started to hurt. But as hard as she tried, as often as she repeated the words Stop it! Stop it! over and over in her head, the rant continued.

"Wot d'ya fink, Jezza? So should I ditch the bitch?"

Well, that clearly hadn't worked. There was only one thing for it.

"Stop it!" she cried, in what she thought was a whisper, but was loud enough for those sitting within several feet of her to hear. They turned to stare at her but she ignored them. "Stop that foul language now, you cretin! And stop saying 'so'!"

The girl opposite looked at her open-mouthed.

But it worked. The teenager emitted a series of animal grunts but no actual words. And it had certainly put paid to the swearing. All that could be heard was the person on the other end of the phone shouting, "I can't hear ya, Inky. Wot ya saying? Speak up. Is you in a tunnel or sumfin'?"

But Inky wasn't in a tunnel although to all intents and purposes he might as well have been. His ability to communicate badly, or indeed at all, had ceased. He shook the phone angrily, stared at the screen, then hit it several times on the back of the seat in front of him. Muttering something that sounded like "Whmph", he gave up and put it in his pocket. There was a collective sigh from the upper deck.

"Blimey, Mrs, I don't know what you just done," said the young girl across the aisle, "but whatever it was, it's shut the bugger up. Respect!"

Lizzie smiled at her. "It has rather, hasn't it?"

"Well done, you!" said, John, taking her hand. "You see. It's not just tv. You can do it in real life too. Oh boy, are we going to have some fun today!"

"Where shall we start?" asked Lizzie.

"I don't know. Let's do our normal shop and see what happens."

"Okay. Coffee first or supermarket?"

John considered the options. "Supermarket then coffee. That's what we'd normally do. We'll just follow our usual routine and see how the day develops. This could be interesting."

Al Fresco's was unusually busy. Normally they could zip round in about twenty minutes, armed with their immutable shopping list - if it's not on the list we don't get it, John was always reminding his wife. They only bought the listed weekly food items, trying hard not to be tempted by all the treats that they once thought they would be able to afford. These days it was special offers that got them excited. But today the queues at the checkouts were unimaginably long as only half a dozen were actually open. By the time they got to the front of the queue, tempers were frayed. Lizzie started to load up the conveyor belt as John went ahead to pack.

"On a go-slow today, are we?" John asked the checkout girl tartly.

She barely looked at him as she slid the first plastic bottle of milk over the sensor. "So it's a lot of people off sick with the flu 'n' stuff."

John looked at his wife who was as yet out of earshot.

"So you haven't weighed your onions." She held a small bag of loose onions in the air.

"Isn't that your job?"

"S'not now. S'yours."

"Since when?"

Lizzie had finished loading and stood beside her husband.

"Since Fursday. So it's all changed now. You have to weigh all your own fruit and veg. So there's new scales and things."

"Nice of you to tell us," said Lizzie sharply, as she got out her card to pay.

The girl shrugged her shoulders as she stared at them. God, she hated this job. She'd rather be working in Tip Top Shop where at least everybody was her age. Not like these old crumblies. She started to speak. Or at least she tried to.

Lizzie and John grinned broadly at each other, finished the packing and paid. They gave each other a high five as they left the store.

⸻

Lizzie and John sat at a small table in the window of The Brew'n'Bun.

"Well, I think that went rather well, don't you?" Lizzie sipped her cappuccino. "That shut the little minx up straight away. I really enjoyed that! Did you see her face! That'll teach her to sneer at us like that!"

"Did you see her pressing the call button as we left? I'd like to see her trying to explain that to her supervisor."

"We're having a good day so far, aren't we? Do you want to try anywhere else?"

"Probably not," John replied. "It's obvious you don't have to shout or even speak to these people any more. I don't think you even have to send any thought waves to them. It seems that they just have to say an unnecessary 'so' in your presence and that's enough."

"Shall we head home?"

"I think so. Quite an exciting day, eh? I can't remember the last time we had so much fun!"

"I'll say! I'll go and settle up." Lizzie walked up to the counter.

"Table 4? So two coffees? That'll be six pounds exactly."

"That's gone up since last time," Lizzie pointed out.

"So, cost of living, don't you..." The man tried to say more but failed. He looked quizzically at Lizzie as she smiled smugly. She turned and left.

John and Lizzie walked slowly to the bus station, heavily laden with bags of shopping.

"I just need to get a paper," John said.

He stopped in front of the newsagent's. "Coming in?" he asked her.

Lizzie nodded. "I always like to see Ahmed. Such a nice man."

"Afternoon Ahmed," said John, picking up a copy of The Yorbridge Yodel and scanning the headlines. "Parking Charges To Rise," it announced. "Bloody hell!" he muttered. "Not again!" He dug a pound coin out of his pocket.

"Good afternoon, Mr Braddon. Good to see you again. You too, missus. Both well?"

Lizzie smiled at him as John replied, "Yes thanks. We're fine. You?"

Ahmed nodded as he gave John his change.

"Oh, and don't forget a lottery ticket, John," prompted Lizzie. She shrugged her shoulders. "You never know."

"A lottery ticket, missus? So I've never known you buy one before. You must be feeling lucky. So Lucky Dip is it?"

Lizzie looked at him. Ahmed grinned pleasantly at her as he handed her a ticket.

"How much is it?" John asked.

Ahmed tried to reply but failed.

John looked aghast. "How much is it?" he asked again.

Ahmed opened his mouth but only managed to produce squeaks. John slammed a fiver down on the counter, picked up the shopping bags and backed out of the shop. Ahmed squeaked after him, fear in his face, waving the fiver.

John marched his wife round the corner, out of sight of the very distressed shop-owner.

"What did you just do?" he hissed.

"Me? I didn't do anything. I just asked for a lottery ticket, that's all. I didn't even speak to the man. I asked you to get it."

"Well, you've probably lost poor Ahmed his livelihood."

"What do you mean?"

"How can the poor bugger sell papers and stuff if he can't talk to his customers? You've really gone and done it now!"

"But I didn't say anything. You were there. I didn't say a word about anything."

John chewed his bottom lip.

Lizzie looked shaken. "It must have been that telepathetic thing you were talking about. That's what must have done it. Poor Ahmed. I wouldn't have done that to him for the world."

John looked intensely at his wife. "You are going to have to be so careful with this."

"Me? You were the one who said we were going to have fun with this today!"

"And we have. Up to a point. But we're just going to have to watch it, that's all."

"Oh John! What are we going to do?"

"I really don't know Lizzie. We need to think about this. Carefully. It's clear that now you don't even have to speak to anyone. Your brain waves are enough to make them stop speaking."

"I'm really scared John. I was really enjoying myself up until this but I don't want to hurt people. Or frighten them. I only want them to stop saying 'so' all the time."

"I want to try this one more time." John looked at his watch. "We've got twenty minutes before the bus goes. Are you game for one more go?"

Lizzie looked dubious. "I'm not sure. What are you thinking?"

"I want to see whether you have to be close enough to hear someone to stop them talking. First of all you shouted at them on live tv and then face-to-face. Now it seems you don't even have to do that. It looks as if it was the power of your mind that made them unable to speak. I want to see if you have to be within earshot of a person or whether you can do it remotely, maybe even through me."

"Don't you think I've done enough harm?"

"This'll tell us exactly what you can and can't do. I think we have to do it."

"What's your plan?"

"I'll go into a shop and buy something. I'll talk to someone. You stay outside. Try to clear your mind. Don't think about anything at all. We've got to see if anything happens if you can't hear or see the person. What do you say?"

Reluctantly, Lizzie nodded. John was right. They had to find out the precise extent of her strange powers in terms of feet and inches so they would know exactly what she was capable of. She followed her husband as he crossed the road and watched him disappear into Bobbits, the hardware and garden shop. John decided he would go and ask about moss-killer; Lizzie would stand in the street, her back to the shop window, just to make sure there was no possibility of her hearing or seeing what was going on inside. Ten minutes later John emerged carrying a bag of All For-Lawn Moss Remover.

"What's that?" asked Lizzie.

"Guy in the shop said it was the best thing for getting rid of moss."

"Any problems?" she asked.

"None at all. The shop assistant must have said 'so' a dozen times. Did you pick up on any of that?"

Lizzie shook her head. "Not a bit. I had my back to you the whole time and didn't think about anything in particular."

"That proves that you alone have to be near enough to overhear and see people then, to have any effect. Interesting."

"But if I affect them only in those circumstances, it means I'm going to have to stay away from people, doesn't it?"

"It looks that way."

"This is getting out of hand, isn't it John? I never expected anything like this to happen. I was having so much fun earlier, stopping all those horrid people saying 'so' all the time. You know how fed up I got with them and just wanted them to stop. Was it too much to ask?"

"I think it may well have been, Lizzie. We'll have to see."

"That wasn't as much fun as I thought it would be," said Lizzie, rubbing her aching feet together. She'd unpacked all the shopping and put it away and was now sitting in the lounge, her feet on the coffee table. "Although that was the quietest bus journey home we've ever had. How many people did I stop talking? Five? Six?"

"Incredible!"

"And all without even thinking about it. It just seems to happen automatically now." She leaned back and massaged her neck. "But what are we going to do?"

"In what respect?" asked John.

"Well it looks as if I have no control over this. I could make most of the population of the town stop talking. Or worse. And what if Elkie or Dan want to come up for a weekend. They both say 'so' all the time. It's always driven me mad but I've never said anything. We can't risk them coming. How can Elkie do her vet work if she can't speak to her clients? Or Dan? I'm never really sure what he does but I know he goes to a lot of meetings. Even abroad." Lizzie paused, thinking deeply. "This could spread round the world and I could be responsible. I've really started something here, haven't I?"

"You certainly have, Lizzie, but I don't know how."

"Me neither. I've never done anything like this before in my life. Do I have special powers, John? Is that what this is?"

"If you can do some sort of magic, I hope you can do better than this."

"Well, we've got that lottery ticket," Lizzie said optimistically.

John smiled. "We have indeed."

"But I need to know if I can undo this. If I can't, who knows what will happen. Shall we see if there's anything on the news about those two from A Country Mile?"

John turned on the tv. A male presenter this time, in a sharp grey suit with a green bow tie, grinned broadly.

"Now for some happy news. I'm delighted to report that Carmen Veranda and Hardy Sole, two tv personalities who mysteriously lost the power of speech whilst on a live edition of our flagship programme, A Country Mile, which reports on all matters rural as I'm sure you know," he took a deep breath, "have been discharged from hospital where they were subject to extensive checks in order to establish what had happened. The hospital has confirmed that both are fit and well and that there is no damage to their vocal chords. It is expected that both will fully recover the power of speech in a very short time. Both send heartfelt thanks - written, of course - to all their fans who have wished them a speedy recovery. And we do too. So the pound has slumped again against the yen..." The news broadcaster looked at the camera as he tried to read from the autocue but nothing happened. His lips flapped ineffectually. A bead of sweat dripped ran down his face as he mouthed an obvious obscenity. Then the screen went blank.

"Lizzie! I was watching that!" remonstrated John.

"Me too!" cried his wife. "I didn't do anything! It just happened. Again! I can't seem to stop it!"

"Let's see if there's anything on ITV."

There was. The local news, North or Thereabouts, had just started. "Strange goings on in Yorbridge today where a number of people apparently lost the power of speech. A sales assistant in the supermarket Al Fresco's seems to have been the first affected. CCTV in the store appears to have shown her discovering this problem as she was dealing with an elderly couple."

"Elderly couple! I like that!" shouted Lizzie. "I am not elderly!"

"This was followed later in the day," the story continued, "by an incident in the Brew'n'Bun coffee shop where a male barista also found himself unable to talk. A further incident occurred at The Hot off the Press newsagent's near the bus station. Our reporter has established, through long and laborious interviews conducted mostly in mime or on paper that, on every occasion, an elderly couple was involved."

"I'm going to write in and complain! How dare they call me elderly!"

"It's not clear how this couple was involved, or if indeed, whether. The Police are making enquiries but have stressed that the public is in no danger. Now over to Jeremy in Saltsea where an unusually high tide last night left the promenade covered in a particularly pungent and slimy seaweed. So Jeremy, this is causing a headache for..." The screen went blank again.

"This is getting tedious, Lizzie."

"Tell me something I don't know! And we thought this was going to be such fun."

For the next few days Lizzie didn't leave the house. She didn't dare. She avoided watching any live tv or listening to any live radio. The house had never been so clean. With a seemingly endless amount of time on her hands, she scrubbed the kitchen floor - twice - cleaned the windows and mirrors, and even had a go at the tiling grout in the bathroom. She read two books - unheard of for her - and, in absolute desperation, arranged the books on the bookshelf according to colour. Come Thursday, she was stir-crazy. She was desperate to leave the house, get some fresh air, but she was terrified of going anywhere where there might be people. Going to the shops was obviously a complete no-no. Even a walk in the park was out of the question. What if she should hear someone saying 'so'? And their weekly trip to the Whispering Ferret was a non-starter. She'd even avoided speaking to Dan and Elkie on the phone in case she inadvertently muzzled her children. John had spoken to them and reassured them that their mother was well; she simply had a slight touch of laryngitis, that was all.

Lizzie wandered aimlessly round the house, straightening pictures, re-folding the bath towels, re-arranging the contents of the kitchen cabinets yet again. If she'd had any idea this was going to happen, she'd have kept quiet about her, how could she describe it? Her annoyance? It was more than that. Bugbear? More than that too. But how could she have known? How could she have possibly guessed that simply by losing her temper over something so trivial, for that's what it was, she would cause such an immediate and widespread debilitating effect upon people?

Once again she found herself watching John from the lounge window as he liberally applied the highly acclaimed moss remover to the front path. Poor John. She'd dragged him into this too. It was affecting his life. The question was, how could they get out of it?

───

The days dragged by. Lizzie had become a prisoner in her own home. She and John could no longer go anywhere together; watching tv together was limited to films and pre-recorded programmes. They couldn't be too careful. Lizzie felt trapped. Was this how it was going to be? She couldn't even go out to do something as mundane as the shopping any more. If she thought her life was dull before, how much worse was it now? Was this how it was going to be? What was worse, she knew she was to blame. The days rolled into weeks - Dan and Elkie were talking of coming to visit so concerned were they about their mother's continuing laryngitis: John had great difficulty persuading them otherwise. The fact that Lizzie and her husband had to spend so much time with each other did nothing to improve matters. With no-one else to talk to, Lizzie vented her frustration on her husband. John put up with it for as long as he could but increasingly sought refuge in the garden. A trip to a supermarket was still possible for him, although after the recent incident, he decided it prudent to give Al Fresco's a miss for the time being. The only benefit to all of this was that the moss was showing signs of finally being licked into shape but he couldn't tell whether it was the wonder product he'd bought from Bobbits or Lizzie's newly-discovered supernatural powers.

Lizzie and John's tedious existence was shattered one afternoon when there was a knock at the door. They'd just finished lunch and were sitting in silence at the kitchen table, John staring at his empty plate, Lizzie contemplating her nails, when they were startled into action.

"Who's that?" asked Lizzie, whispering.

"Only one way to find out." John stood up.

"Be careful!" warned his wife.

"Of what?" demanded John.

John opened the front door to reveal two men on the doorstep. The older man was dressed in a suit, the other, jeans and a jacket.

"Mr Braddon?" asked the older of the two.

John nodded. "Yes."

"Mr John Braddon?"

Lizzie peered out from behind the kitchen door. Visitors were a rare occurrence but since their last trip to the shops together, there had been none.

"I'm Inspector Watson and this is Sergeant Singh from Yorbridge Police."

Hearing the word 'Police', Lizzie feared the worst. She ran down the hallway. "What's happened?" she cried. "Is it Dan? Elkie? Who's been hurt?"

"And you must be Mrs Braddon. No-one's hurt, we'd just like to have a chat with you. Mind if we come in?"

Lizzie sighed with relief. At least the children were safe.

"Please," said John, showing them into the lounge. "Have a seat. Tea? Coffee?"

"No thanks. This won't take too long."

John sat in one of the armchairs whilst Lizzie hovered in the doorway.

"Won't you join us, Mrs Braddon?"

She shuffled in and perched on the arm of her husband's chair.

"What's all this about?" she squeaked nervously.

"We're making enquiries into several incidents that happened in Yorbridge a few weeks ago."

John cast a sideways glance at his wife. "What sort of incidents?" he asked.

"Well, it's rather strange, but quite a few people seem to have lost the ability to speak."

"And what's that got to do with us?" asked John.

"From what we can establish, with CCTV footage and speaking to witnesses, you and your wife appear to be the common denominator."

"How dare you!" shouted an indignant Lizzie. "I am not common!"

"Sshh," said John.

"First they call me old! Now they call me common! I will not put up with it!"

"Perhaps my choice of words was not the best," said Inspector Watson. "What I'm trying to say is, that on every occasion when someone became unable to talk, you and your husband were involved."

"Involved? I don't understand. How? Are you saying that we were to blame?" Lizzie cried. "I've never heard anything so preposterous in my life!"

"Preposterous it may be," said Sergeant Singh, "the facts speak for themselves. A young sales assistant in Al Fresco stopped talking when you shouted at her..."

"I did not shout at her," said Lizzie angrily. "I merely...remonstrated with her. She was being rude."

"And then a man in Brew'n'Bun, a barista, I believe that's what they're called, was able to describe you - on paper of course. And then there was a Mr Ahmed Khan in the newsagent's. He knows you by name. It was while you were in his shop that he stopped speaking. Oh, and he asked - or rather wrote - asking us to tell you that he owes you £3. Apparently you gave him too much money for the lottery ticket? And then there's all the people on the bus."

"What bus?" asked Lizzie disingenuously.

"The one you caught home," said Sergeant Singh. "From Yorbridge. At least 8 people reported a loss of speech to their doctors, 6 from one surgery alone. In view of the large number, the surgery rang us to notify us in case it was part of a wider epidemic."

"As many as 8," Lizzie muttered to herself.

"Would you like to tell us what's going on?" said the Sergeant.

"There's nothing going on," said John. "The fact that a few people aren't able to talk has got nothing to do with us. And even if it did, what's the crime?"

"Good question," replied the Inspector. "And to be honest, I'm not sure I know the answer. But depriving a person of their right to speech may well be a criminal offence."

"Poppycock! We haven't denied anybody their right to free speech."

"I didn't say free speech, I just said speech."

"That makes even less sense," said John.

"Whatever it is, we'd like it to stop," said the Inspector.

"And you don't think I wouldn't?" asked Lizzie.

"Are you involved then?"

"No, of course she's not," said John.

"But what if it doesn't stop?" asked Lizzie. "Would you arrest me?" She thrust her hands out at the policeman. "Go on! I dare you! Handcuff me!"

"So I don't think it will come to tha..!" Inspector Watson stopped mid-sentence. He gargled a few words, fear written all over his face.

"What have you done?" asked Sergeant Singh.

Lizzie looked aghast. "I haven't done anything," she whimpered.

"That's exactly what happened to everyone we interviewed. One minute they could speak and the next they couldn't. What are you doing?"

"Nothing. It's not me!" Lizzie was close to tears. "I can't help it!"

"Help what?"

"I can't control it!" Tears were pouring down her face. Was this what a confession felt like?

"Control what?" The Sergeant looked at his boss whose face was a picture of despair. Inspector Watson was trying to speak but all that came out were strange noises and lots of spit.

"When someone says 'so' when they shouldn't, they stop being able to talk," explained Lizzie.

"I don't understand. If someone says 'so' when they shouldn't you can make them stop talking?"

Lizzie nodded.

"But I just said it and nothing happened. I can still speak."

"You used it correctly. There's a difference."

"This is crazy!" Sergeant Singh's voice had risen an octave.

"Perhaps you'd both like a nice cup of tea now," suggested John, trying to defuse the situation.

"Tea? So I don't think..."

There! It had happened again. The police officers looked at one another. Speechless, John looked at his wife.

"Did you have to do that?" he hissed.

She shrugged and wiped her eyes. "Nothing to do with me. It just happens, remember?"

The two policemen stood up. Inspector Watson scrabbled in his pocket for a pen and wrote something in his notebook. He tore off the sheet and gave it to Lizzie. 'We'll be back!' it read. Lizzie showed it to her husband. John nodded.

"I rather expect you will," he said.

"Well the cat is well and truly out of the bag now," said John grimly, as he closed the door on the mute policemen.

"But I can't see we've committed any crime. What harm have we done?"

John laughed. "It's ironic, isn't it! Preventing people from a right to free speech may be a crime but just stopping them talking is not! What a world we live in! You can say pretty much exactly what you like but you've got to have the ability to physically say it! Crazy!"

"And what do we do now?" Lizzie asked her husband. "Any suggestions?"

"Not one!"

"Do you think going to the doctor might help? Me, I mean."

"Maybe. But I'm not sure what a doctor could do. It's not as if you've got a recognisable medical condition. Maybe you had a mental condition when you willed people to stop using the S word. But now all that has to happen is for you to be near someone for them to stop talking. I can't see how a doctor can fix that."

"There has to be a way," insisted Lizzie. "What about hypnotism?"

"I don't know. Maybe it could re-wire your brain so that you don't get excited about people who use the S word wrongly, but bearing in mind you only have to be close to someone for them to go dumb, I'm not sure that that would work either."

"I don't want to go to prison."

"That's not going to happen," John reassured her. "We just need to come up with a plan, that's all."

"That's easy for you to say," said Lizzie. "I'm the guilty party here. This is all down to me."

John took her hand. "We're both in this together," he said. "We're a team, remember?" He kissed her on the cheek. "I'm going out to the garden." He stopped and looked at her. "You didn't do anything about the moss, did you?"

"What do you mean?"

"Well, it's disappearing, that's all. I wondered if you'd had a word with it or something!"

"A moss whisperer, you mean? No, John," Lizzie laughed. "It's nothing to do with me. Must be that stuff you got from town."

John said nothing but he wasn't convinced.

Lizzie spent the rest of the day fretting. Had she committed a crime? Was it against the law to stop someone talking? She'd done it for what, maybe a dozen people and that was only because they used the S word when they shouldn't have. How could that be breaking the law? Another thought crossed her mind. Even if it wasn't against the law could those people sue her? For what? Personal injury? Did all those people even know that she was to blame? Ahmed probably did. But the rest of them? Had the police told each and every one of them whom they suspected? She smiled. Those two policeman wouldn't be telling anyone anything anytime soon! But it wasn't funny. It really wasn't. Could she really be sued? Lizzie shuddered at the thought. They had no money, she and John. They would have to sell the bungalow. It was the only thing they had. Where would they go? How would they live? Oh, why had she let such a silly little thing take over her life? Why hadn't she just ignored what people said, how they spoke? It really didn't matter in the great scheme of things, did it? What was it John had been saying all along? Go with the flow. But she couldn't leave it alone, could she? Big deal if someone used the S word when they shouldn't. There were worse crimes. And what had it achieved? Absolutely nothing, Lizzie told herself. She hadn't been able to speak to her children for weeks now. She didn't dare leave the house to go shopping. Or the pub. Or anywhere for that matter. What sort of life was this for her? For them both? It had been a bit of fun in the beginning but it certainly wasn't any more. Lizzie was exhausted with it all. She lay down on the sofa which is where John found her, an hour later, fast asleep.

"Are you okay?" he asked, as she opened her eyes. "Here, I made you a cuppa."

Lizzie burst into tears.

"What's the matter?"

"Everything! All this stupid business. Why couldn't I leave it well alone! I'm either going to go to prison or lots of people are going to sue me."

"That's not going to happen. I promise you."

"We're going to end up homeless and all because of me." Her sobbing continued unabated. "Oh John, what have I done?"

"You haven't done anything except maybe make some annoying people be quiet for a bit. And I can't for the life of me see how that's a crime. In fact, there's probably a lot of people who would appreciate what you've done, if only they knew."

"Do you really mean that?"

"Of course I do."

"But I can't speak to Dan or Elkie in case I put the curse on them!" She sighed deeply and sipped her tea. "Thank you for standing by me, John."

"What else would I do? You're my wife and I love you. We'll come through this. Don't worry. And we're not going to end up homeless."

Lizzie sat up, drying her eyes. "I've been such an idiot, haven't I?"

"Impatient maybe. Intolerant definitely. But an idiot? No. And don't forget, you didn't really do anything. This thing seemed to have taken on a life of its own. You were only a channel, if you like. The means to let this thing happen."

"Like John Hurt in Alien? When that thing burst out of his stomach, you mean?"

John smiled broadly. "Sort of. But not as messy."

"What do we do now then?"

"We wait. We wait to see if the police come back. We wait to see if the pair from A Country Mile programme get their voices back. And Ahmed of course. And we must check that lottery ticket. Who knows? We could be sitting on a small fortune."

"Knowing our luck, I don't think so. We've never won anything. Ever. No, this thing has been nothing but a curse." Lizzie looked pensive. "Maybe I am a witch?"

"A witch?" John squeezed her hand. "You are not a witch, Lizzie Braddon."

"How do you know? Nothing like this has ever happened to me before. Maybe somehow I've suddenly become a wicked witch and this is only the start of it. I could be putting all sorts of spells on people whenever they annoy me."

"I can't explain it, Lizzie. I doubt if anyone can. But one thing's for sure. You are not a witch. And we're going to get this thing sorted."

"Promise?"

"I promise."

Lizzie smiled at her husband. Please, let him be right.

Another week went by and there were still no further visits from the police. Lizzie hadn't really expected there to be – if the pair from A Country Mile were still not able to talk, and it was over a month ago since her outburst at the television that had rendered them both speechless, then she didn't expect the police would be in a position to interview her anytime soon. John had visited Ahmed's paper shop on his last shopping trip to Yorbridge. The man could still not speak but seemed to bear no grudges as he'd handed John a copy of The Yorbridge Yodel along with the £3 he owed them, even smiling as he did so. John had taken the money but felt so guilty about everything that he immediately stuffed it in the collection tin for the local Homes for Hedgehogs Scheme. Al Fresco's was still forbidden territory as far as he was concerned but the new low budget supermarket, Low'n'Local, that had just opened near the park, was an adequate substitute. And cheaper.

On Sunday evening John was watching the local evening news on his own whilst Lizzie was in the kitchen organising the tins in her cupboards into date order.

"You might want to come and see this," he shouted from the lounge.

"What is it?"

"Quick, Lizzie! Local news. An item about the Country Mile pair."

Lizzie stood in the doorway, frightened to get any closer to the tv.

"Good news for the Country Mile Clams, as they've been named locally," announced a young man sitting at a desk, the North or Thereabouts sign brightly illuminated behind him. "Following an incident at Hardy Sole's farm on a live edition of A Country Mile, when the actor and a presenter were left speechless whilst on air, the programme makers are delighted to announce that both have fully recovered the power of speech. We spoke to Hardy earlier today."

"No doubt this has been the most worrying time of my life. I mean, as an actor, it's imperative that I speak - unless I was doing a silent movie, not that there's much call for that these days to be honest! Ha ha! For the last month I have been extremely concerned that I may never act again."

"I didn't know you ever had," said John. Lizzie crept into the room and stood behind her husband. She rested her hand on his shoulder, hardly daring to breathe.

"But now I have my voice back, I'm thrilled. I, we, that is, Carmen and I, have no idea what happened or what caused us to lose our ability to talk, but we have been made aware that locally several others, possibly as many as dozens, may have been similarly afflicted. It's all a mystery. But we assume that since we can speak again, they will be able to too." He smiled broadly straight into the camera.

Lizzie let out a long sigh. "Thank God!" She clapped her hands in joy. "Is it really over, John?"

"It certainly sounds like it."

"And that means I can go out and even if I do make people near me lose the power of speech, they'll get it back in a few weeks? They'll be able to talk. It won't be a permanent thing?"

"That's what it looks like," said John.

"Phew!" said Lizzie. "You have no idea how relieved I am."

John squeezed her hand as they both turned their attention back to the tv.

"What about the rumours that this was, like, some sort of curse?" continued the news reporter, a young girl who looked to be about 14. "Like, by a witch."

"I had heard that, but to be honest, we don't have curses in this day and age, do we? Nor witches. No, it's just one of life's little mysteries. No real harm done, eh?"

"I must admit, that's very magna...magnanim...big of you, especially, like, some people had suggested that an old woman might have been involved. Sounds like a witch, like."

"God, I hate it when they do that!" said Lizzie, gripping her husband's hand so hard he winced.

"Do what?" asked John.

"Say 'like' all the time. It really bugs me. And she called me old! Some people have no respect!"

John stood up and turned the tv off. He faced his wife, hands on hips. "Lizzie, don't go there! Don't you dare even think about it!"

"Think about what?" his wife asked indignantly. "It's not good, that's all I'm saying. Using 'like' like that. It's so wrong. Shows a lack of education if you ask me."

"I don't care what you think, Lizzie. Forget you even heard it!"

"Easier said than done, John. And you know what happened last time."

"Oh boy, do I!"

Lizzie stared at her husband, smiling mischievously.

"What?"

She giggled. "I had you going there, didn't I?"

"Oh, very funny, Lizzie." He shook his head. "Please don't do that to me."

"But it was fun, wasn't it? For a while at least. And I did shut up all those dreadful people. And we did have a bit of a laugh. We don't seem to have done that for a long time."

"We did have a laugh. But not much and not for long. But enough is enough. No more. Promise?"

Lizzie didn't reply.

"Promise?" he repeated, threateningly. "Remember the police? How upset you got? Thinking you were going to jail? Or going to be sued? I think we've both had plenty of excitement for a while."

"You're right, John. I think I've had enough distraction to last me for a long time yet."

"Speaking of excitement, Lizzie, do we still have that lottery ticket? I can't remember where I put it."

"Here. It's in my purse. I put it there for safe-keeping."

John took it from her and looked on his phone for the lottery results.

"No. No good I'm afraid. We didn't win."

"Did you really expect us to?"

"No. I suppose not. As you say, we never win anything. But I was hoping you had some of those magic powers left," he said, laughing.

"I thought you said I wasn't a witch."

John shrugged his shoulders. "You're not. But who's to say I'm not wrong? Maybe you could find a teeny, little power from somewhere. Nothing big. Just enough to change our fortunes around. Think you can manage that?"

Lizzie shook her head, smiling. "You do talk daft sometimes, you know."

"Maybe we should try again next week?" suggested John.

"Waste of money. We won't win, so why waste our money?"

John was about to tear up the ticket and put it in the recycling bin.

"Hang on, John. Are you sure you checked the right date? It was over a month ago we bought it."

"No. You're right. I did it for yesterday."

John keyed in the correct date. He looked at Lizzie then looked at his phone again. "Lizzie, check this for me, will you?"

Lizzie looked at him. "Why?"

"You have to get 6 numbers, don't you?"

"I think so."

"You know when I asked if you could find a little magical power…?"

5
POPPADOMS

...

I'm waiting to die. Well, no. That's not quite true. They are waiting for me to die. This lot. The ones sat round the table. My family. They're waiting for me to head off to the other side. My slack-arsed son, his slap-thighed wife and the improbable fruit from their unimaginable loins. They are quietly waiting for me to go. I'm in the way, you see. A nuisance. An embarrassment. It's not that I'm incontinent or anything like that. And I don't dribble. It's just that I'm old. No real use any more. At least that's what they think. Time for me to go. Shuffle off this mortal coil or whatever and let them get on with their lives. They're probably right. The only problem, for them anyway, is that I've got a bit more life left in me. Quite a lot, in fact. And I've got the wherewithal to make the most of it. Oh, didn't I mention I'm quite wealthy? Really quite wealthy in fact. And that's another reason they want me to go.

Anyway, we're sitting in the Bombay Duck Restaurant on the High Street. It's May Bank Holiday. Last night I got a call from Robert, my son. He's the one sat opposite me. Robert, you note, not Bobby. Or Robbie. Which is what we used to call him when he was little. Somewhere along the line he got arsey and decided that only Robert would do. Believe me, he's got nothing to be arsey about.

"We want to take you out for a meal tomorrow, Mum," he'd said. "Bit of a treat. Haven't seen you in a while." All good things must come to an end, I suppose. "Thought you might be a bit lonely. Like to go out? See the kids? Actually it was Lettuce's suggestion." I bet. "I think we ought to take your mum out for dinner, she said. Those were her very words." I can hear them now. Ah, Lettuce. My wide-hipped, witless daughter-in-law.

Lettuce isn't her real name, of course. It's Leticia. Don't ask! Sounds more like a sneeze. How could any sane parent in this day and age call their daughter Leticia? And how could any sane person in this day and age give her the nickname Lettuce? I know the answer to that one – my son! And of course it was her suggestion we go out for dinner. Take the old bag out. Keep her sweet. I'm not daft. At least, not as daft as they think I am. And while I'm introducing you to my family, that's Kaylea, my granddaughter. That's right. That's how they spell it. They call her Lea for short so I call her Kale. I'm not being awkward or anything, calling her Kale. Well, maybe just a little. I know how much it annoys them. But if we've got a lettuce in the family, why not a cabbage too? And then there's Damien, my grandson. What sort of name is that? Sounds like something out of a horror film. Or an MP. As usual, he's got his nose buried in a computer game. One that's meant to increase your brain power. As if. We're in a restaurant for goodness' sake! Couldn't he leave the wretched thing at home for once and try some intelligent conversation? Obviously not.

"You're a bit sniffy, Gran," says Kale. Too bloody right. Got every reason to be with a family like mine. "Have you got a cold?"

You wish! I expect she's hoping it's the start of something terminal that'll see me off in days. Hah! I'm in the best of health! Never fitter. Bad news for her. For all of them. I know she's got her eye on a second-hand car. 16 and wanting a car! She'll have to wait a long time yet if I have anything to do with it.

"No, I don't think I have," I reply sweetly. See, I can do it if I try. "Well, maybe. Perhaps it's the start of a summer cold." I sniffed giving some credence to the idea. Let's give her some hope. "We'll see."

She turns back to the menu.

The Bombay Duck isn't bad as Indian restaurants go, although I know you get a far better curry at The Cardamom Caper. Although neither of them is really Indian. They never are. It doesn't have that dreadful red flock wallpaper. Nor that piercing whiny music that sounds like a wasp in a bottle. No. The walls are a nice shade of lilac with some delightful woodcuts. And the tables are nicely laid with white linen tablecloths although the serviettes are paper. Even so, I wonder how much bleach they get through here. Someone is going to spill something or dribble and you can guarantee it will be bilious and vomit-coloured. And I like the way they show you to your table here. Not the over-the-top bowing and grovelling as if you'd just come from the Gymkhana Club with your pith helmet in one hand and your dhobi-wallah in the other. No sycophancy here. Just plain good manners. A polite "Good Evening, Madam/Sir", and a pleasant young man who leads you to your table. None of this shaking your serviette with a flourish and putting it in your lap. I can manage that myself. The menus are already on the table.

"What would you like to drink, Mum?" Robert asks me.

"I would like a glass of wine please. Shall we get a bottle?"

I'm not supposed to see the look that passes between him and Lettuce.

"What about a jug of lassi and some water?" he replies.

Then why bloody ask?

"Fine," I say. Tightwads.

Actually I hate that yogurt stuff. That's for invalids. Not a drink to have with dinner. Robert orders the drinks from the hovering waiter.

"A jug of mango lassi and a jug of water please. And five glasses."

"Mineral water?" asks the waiter. As if.

"Tap will do."

"Would you like any poppadoms?" asks the waiter.

"I don't think so," says Robert.

"I do," I say. I don't really like them but I'm making a point here. Robert and Leticia look at me. I smile back and nod at them both.

"Ok," says Robert. "We'll have two. We can share."

Push the boat out why don't you! I smile again. Small victory.

"What do you fancy eating, Mum?" Leticia asks me.

I am not your mother. I'm your mother-in-law. It's not that I hate her. I just can't see the point of her.

"I fancy a lamb rogan josh."

"Lamb can be a bit chewy," says Robert. What he means is that lamb is the most expensive item on the menu. And what if it is a bit tough? I've still got my own teeth. Well, most of them. "Why not have chicken?"

Because I bloody well want lamb!

"Ok," I concede. "I'll have chicken." What's the point?

The waiter brings the drinks and starts to pour the semi-liquid mango goo. I put my hand over my glass.

"None for me, thank you."

"Don't you like it?" asks Kale. I shake my head and wrinkle my nose. "I think it's wicked!" she says.

Wicked? Wicked? Of course it is.

"Have the rest of you decided what you want?" Robert asks his family.

They nod. The waiter produces a pad from his back pocket and licks the stub of his pencil he's found behind his ear.

"I'll have a chicken korma," says Leticia.

Bland is as bland does. Nothing too spicy. She doesn't know the meaning of the word.

I opt for a chicken dopiaza, Robert, a chicken balti and the youths, chicken biryanis. A tough day for fowl.

"Would you like any rice with that?" asks our waiter. "Any bread – naan, chapattis?"

"How about a family naan?" asks Robert. Value for money, eh?

The waiter repeats our order to make sure it's correct and leaves us. We can see him in the kitchen through a wide glass window as he tears the order from his pad and places it on a spike. One of the chefs takes it off, reads it and throws something into an over-sized wok. Sweat pours from his brow and drops into the highly-spiced concoction. Extra flavour, I suppose.

I look round the restaurant. It's still early yet and only one other table is occupied. Like ours, it's in the window, fronting on to the High Street. Makes the place look busy and popular. The other diners are a middle–aged couple. He's dressed in faded jeans and matching shirt. She's in beige crimplene. Tasty! Why do people wear clothes like that? He must be 55 if he's a day, with a beer gut and thinning on top. Hair swept from under his armpit to hide his bald patch. She's not much better. Thick make-up trying to hide a bad skin. Cheap blond highlights. And from where I sit, I can see rolls of stomach squashed together under the table, her serviette doing a poor job of hiding them. She's seen better days. But then, haven't we all?

The waiter brings the poppadoms and a selection of garish sauces and pickles in a stainless steel server. The youths leap in, breaking off pieces of the large, pale crisp. Small pools of fat wallow in the hollows. Robert grabs the plate and proffers it to me. I snap a bit off the poppadom and put it on my plate with some of the pickle and what looks like throat clearings but I know is mint yogurt. We eat in silence except for the odd crunch and slurp. We finish eating and no-one says anything. The couple at the other table haven't talked at all. They hardly even look at each other. Must be married.

"What have you been up to at school, Kale?" I ask in an attempt at conversation.

She's doing her GCSEs this year and wants to leave school straight after. Wants to go to college to do 'Beauty'. Has an ambition to work in a Nail Salon. Why not just die now and cut out the crap in the middle?

"Same old, same old, Gran," she replies.

Same old what? It's not even English. And she used to be such a sweet thing. Pretty too. Now she spends all her time texting her equally vacuous friends and reading girl magazines. I say 'girl' but I hardly think that covers it. I picked one up last time I was invited to their house. I don't call it a home as it lacks soul. Bit like them. 'Girl Power' it was called. Glossy paper covered in ads for nail varnish and panty liners. It had features too. One was 'Position of the Week'. Position of the Week? That must mean there are 52 positions. At least. And I thought there was only one. There was a drawing of a couple having sex. At least I think that's what they were doing. I showed the magazine to her mother.

"Do you think it right your daughter reads stuff like this?"

Lettuce had looked at the picture and shrugged. Frigid old coot, I could hear her thinking.

"If she didn't read about it in magazines, she'd hear all about it from her friends."

"And that doesn't worry you?"

She shrugged again. I could slap her. "She's a sensible girl. She can always come to me for advice about contraception."

"Contraception? She's 16 for goodness' sake!"

"Oh, they're all doing it."

What! Your daughter is a little slapper. With beautiful nails, certainly. But still a slapper. Don't you care? But of course, I didn't say that. I didn't say anything at all.

The poppadoms finished, the waiter clears the plates. We sit. Nobody speaks. I look at Robert. How can I have given birth to this lump of lard in front of me, raised him for I don't know how many years, seen him leave home, get married and have children, and I can find nothing to say to him, nor him to me. We have nothing in common. Other than genes. And those are faded. Silence. The only sounds come from the kitchen. We wait for our chicken.

"So are you keeping well?" asked Robert, making an effort. I nod. "What have you been up to?"

"Oh, this and that."

"Heard from Dad at all?" he asks tentatively. I glare at him.

"Your father and I have nothing to do with each other. I have not spoken to him since he left me for that silly little tart who runs the fish and chippy on the sea front."

"Mum! Language, please!" cried Lettuce.

I turn to Lettuce. She wilts under my gaze.

"My husband of thirty-seven years left me for some little trollop who couldn't keep her knickers on. With a face like a horse's arse and the IQ of a coffee table. I will say what I want!"

"Mum!" Robert this time. "Please! Not in front of the children."

I look at Kale and Damien. They're loving it. Never heard me swear like this before.

"No, Robert. I will say what I think. Your father is a bastard. A cold-hearted, small-minded shit of a man. Who left me when he got bored."

"But he's still my dad," whines Robert.

"He may well be. But he's not my husband."

I don't know why I'm making such a song and dance about this. Truth to tell, the day he left me, I hung out the flags. Metaphorically. Best thing that ever happened to me. And, even better, I got the house. And a sizeable chunk of his money. He's now slumming it in a tiny flat above his lady-friend's chip shop, smelling of stale fat and old fish. And that's just her. And now I'm rich. I played the poor abandoned wife in the divorce courts with gusto. Aplomb. Took him to the cleaners. And how! And what with the money I'd carefully saved over the years and my settlement, I'm happy. Very.

"I'm going to sell the house," I inform them.

At that moment the chicken dishes arrive. And the over-sized naan bread. I start to spoon some of the lumpy orange sauce onto my plate. Nobody else even looks at their food. They are too busy looking at me.

"But you can't do that. It's the family home."

"Was," I correct him.

Robert sees the house – and his inheritance – disappearing before his very eyes.

"It's too big for little old me on my own." Pathetic but effective.

"But where will you live?" asks Lettuce, alarmed.

"I thought I might come and live with you," I say mischievously. They gawp. Priceless.

"I wouldn't get so lonely then." Milking this for all it was worth. Hadn't had so much fun in days. Robert gulps.

"Are you serious?"

"Absolutely."

All four look at me, mouths agape, chicken getting cold.

"But we don't have the room," says Lettuce.

"I'm sure we could manage." Then I laugh. "Perhaps the children could share a bedroom?"

The looks from Damien and Kale said it all. If I died on the spot they couldn't have been happier! This was such fun!

"Don't worry. I'm only teasing. I wouldn't do that to you." I smile at them all. All four smile back. I could hear the collective sigh of relief. Crisis averted. I eat a piece of chicken. Tasteless, despite the fluorescent sauce.

"We could move in with you," suggests Robert. "It's a big house and it would mean keeping it in the family." Kerching!

"Oh no. I couldn't ask that of you. So much upheaval for you all." If the sarcasm was any thicker it would match what was on the plate in front of me. "No. I've made up my mind, Robert. Too many painful memories." I can lie so well. But am I lying? I can't remember more than a handful of happy days spent there with my husband – ex-husband – and son.

"So what will you do?" asks Robert. "Where will you go?"

"Will you go into a home?" asks Damien. This is the first time he's spoken to me all evening. "Like for old people? "Ouch!" Clearly someone has kicked him under the table.

I glare at him. He suddenly finds his biryani incredibly interesting.

"No, that wouldn't suit me at all. They're full of old people. Wee and dribble. No, I'm not ready for that yet."

"Are you going to buy somewhere else, then?" asked Robert. That at least would keep some of his inheritance intact. I wonder if he can even spell the word. I nod. The waiter appears.

"Is everything alright with the chicken?" he asks, concerned. Nobody except me has touched their food.

"Delicious," I lie.

He goes away, not convinced. The others start to eat.

"I've got somewhere in mind," I tell Robert.

"Somewhere close?" he asks. I smile broadly. I am enjoying this.

"Not really," I say.

"What sort of place is it?" asks Kale.

"Mobile."

"Mobile! You're going to live in a caravan?" asks Lettuce. "Brill!"

"Not as such."

"I don't understand," says Robert. But then you never did.

"I'm going to live on a boat."

"A boat?" they cry in unison.

"Like on one of those canal boats?" asks Kale. "A longboat? Wicked!"

I shake my head.

"I think you'll find they're called narrow boats. Longboats are what the Vikings sailed in." History not a feature in her school, then. "No. This one moves about a lot quicker."

"You planning on sailing round the world?" asks Damien. "Cool!" He laughs.

Someone my age doing something so ridiculous!

"I am." That stops them in their tracks. "Except I'm not going to be doing the sailing."

Oh, this is such fun. I am torturing them.

"What exactly do you mean, Mother?" Mother?

I produce a glossy brochure from my handbag and put it on the table. On the front is an oversized cruise liner sailing in an impossibly blue sea with a matching sky. 'Your Life at Sea' it says. Robert picks it up and stares.

"I am going to buy a cabin on this ship and spend the rest of my life sailing round and round the world."

I am smug. I've never done smug before and I like it.

"But these things are incredibly expensive," says Robert. 'I mean, eye-wateringly expensive.'

"Oh, I know."

"Can you afford it?"

"I can now. Thanks to your father. There'll be nothing left for you, I'm afraid. Or the grandchildren. The cost of buying the cabin is huge. And the service charges are quite extortionate." I shrug my shoulders in silent apology. "But you wouldn't want your poor old mum to miss out on what's going to be a very long and happy retirement, would you? Not after all I've been through?"

Robert coughs and looks at his wife. "No, of course not," he squeaks. "It's a wonderful idea." His face is going purple.

"I knew you'd approve," I say. "Now, how about some ice-cream?"

"I think we'd better give that a miss," says Robert. "Got to watch the pennies, you know."

I can only agree.

6
THREE SHETLAND PONIES

Sorry!

I hope you haven't started to read this story in the expectation of a delightful tale about three Shetland ponies, with their come-hither eyes peeking out from flowing manes, and their rotund Thelwellian bellies, girths stretched to near-breaking point, or their chubby little arses, farting rhythmically as they canter comically round a paddock. If that's the case, then I'm afraid you're going to be very disappointed. You see, I've only included them in my story as a means of comparison. Confused? You won't be.

How many times have you seen something compared in size with six double-decker buses, for example? Or heard about something whose area is the size of Wales? Well why not something the size of three Shetland ponies? Imagine them, these cartoonish characters stacked on top of one another. Could be the height of an elephant. Or a famous London landmark, though nothing immediately springs to mind. But it doesn't necessarily have to be something physical. Why couldn't a situation or an incident be worthy of one, two or even three, Shetland ponies? What I'm trying to say is that this is a tale about size. Now I know what you're thinking so I'll stop you right there! Honestly! Some people! No, this is a story of the magnitude of my life. Not all of it, obviously, but a very important bit. You see, looking back, my life started out very small and stayed that way for quite a long time. What's a small life? I hear you ask. It's one where nothing very much happens often. Mine had been nothing special. Nothing huge had ever happened to me or to anyone close to me, not that there are that many of those, except for my Mum and Dad and my sister. I was born. I lived my life quietly and in my own small way and, one day, I expected to die in the same manner. And that was about the size of it. Or so I thought.

...

First of all let me introduce myself. My name's Rob. It's a small name or at least I think so. I mean, I know it's small in length, being only three letters long, but it's small in magnitude if you know what I mean. My full name is actually Robson Harvey James but I've always been called Rob. I'm quite happy that there's nothing grand about the name and I think it suits me because it's unpretentious. Not that I'm saying all Robs have small lives. I'm sure some have done wonderful things in their time. It's just that I haven't. I'd like to have found a cure for arthritis or hopped from Pole to Pole. But of course I didn't. My biggest achievement to date? I did make a cheese soufflé once. And only once. Don't ask me why. I don't usually do much cooking – not a big fan. But for some unexplained reason I got it into my head that I had to make a cheese soufflé. Maybe it was one of those things on my non-existent bucket list. So I did. I made one and I was very proud of it at the time. And still am, come to think of it. I went out and bought all the ingredients – I didn't have many of them in the flat which I think tells you plenty about my culinary skills. No eggs. No cheese. Although I did have some butter. I followed the recipe to the letter and do you know what? It was perfect. The recipe said eat it immediately so I did as I was told. Unfortunately as there was no-one to share it with, I had to eat the whole damn thing at one sitting. Wouldn't recommend it. It's not something I'll be repeating, unlike the soufflé which seemed to stay with me for days after. But you see what I mean about small.

I mentioned my flat there. Perhaps if I tell you about my circumstances you'll understand why I think my life is small. Shouldn't take too long.

I live in a one bed flat above an off-licence close to the town centre. It's handy as I can walk to work. It would be even handier if I drank. But I don't. Well, not any more. It's a pleasant enough place and I rent it from Ahmed who owns the premises. He's a good bloke. As long as the rent's paid on time (which it always is) he doesn't bother me. The flat's spread over two floors. The first comprises a surprisingly large lounge with a kitchen tucked away in an alcove. There's a tiny bathroom off to one side, then up a narrow flight of stairs to the bedroom, up in the attic with sloping ceilings. I have to be careful not to bang my head when I get up in the morning. I've been here for nearly two years now and have got it just the way I want it. Which is to say it's pretty much as it was on the day I moved in. Pale grey walls, dark grey curtains. A rug on the floor between the sofa and the tv. The kitchen is compact and has a small table with two chairs which I use alternatively so they both get their fair share of wear. The few kitchen cabinets are grey and are mostly empty – when you live on your own you don't need much in the way of pots and pans – especially if you don't cook. There's a small fridge-freezer (where I keep my butter) next to the sink. I don't need a washing machine as there's a launderette just around the corner. It's interesting that I describe the kitchen as compact rather than small. There's a huge difference. It's the polite way of saying it's tiny, which it is. And it feels pinched. But I would never describe my life that way. I suppose they both have their limitations, the flat and my life, but they both work for me. I don't feel that either restrict me in any way. Both suit me just fine.

Upstairs, there's a double bed in the bedroom – just – a small chest of drawers and a flat-pack wardrobe housing my very limited clothing. Jeans. Shirts. Trainers. Not exactly what you'd call haute couture. But it's me to a T shirt. The window from my lounge overlooks a street which is rendered impassable, and therefore quiet, by all the double-parked cars, and the window at the back overlooks a narrow alleyway full of overflowing bins. But you'll have to take my word for that. Although the windows are double-glazed, the panels have long-since blown which means my outlook on the world is opaque and out of focus. Quite apt, I think. The skylight in my bedroom is the same and presents a fuzzy view of the heavens above. Which sits with my view of religion nicely. Still, it filters whatever light there is and saves the need for a curtain.

Don't get me wrong. I'm not looking for sympathy. The place suits me down to the ground. It's small, I know, but I don't need anything grander, and it's easy to keep clean and tidy – I don't have many possessions and I know how to use a duster. And it's not as if I do any entertaining or anything like that. I watch a lot of tv – who doesn't? And I use the kitchen sparingly. Cooking toast – one of my favourite meals – doesn't make much of a mess. So the place is neat. And functional. And for me, it's home. It also has the added advantage of being affordable. Which is just as well on my salary. Salary, I hear you say. Not wages? No. I get a salary. I'll tell you about my job in a bit.

I left home after sixth form college. I'd done pretty well in school. Everyone called me a swot but I was just interested in learning things. With few friends to distract me I'd concentrated on my studies and got decent grades both in school and college. There was even talk of university but my parents could never have afforded it and I didn't know what I wanted to study, if anything, so I decided I'd better get a job. Which, strangely enough, proved to be easier than I thought. I'd had casual jobs throughout my secondary education – small jobs that paid matching wages – but they provided me with pocket money for my non-existent hobbies. Yes, the pittances I earned from stacking shelves in supermarkets, being a waiter in a pizza parlour, helping out in the kitchen in a pub (which might explain my lack of interest in food and cooking – I've sliced enough carrots to last me a lifetime), yes, all these wages went untouched. I had nothing to spend them on. I'm not interested in football – City can sink or swim as far as I'm concerned. In fact I don't like any sport and am not too keen on the great outdoors. To be perfectly honest, I'm not too keen on the great indoors either! I don't really go anywhere. Or do anything much. I've been to the cinema. Even went to a gig once. Not terribly exciting eh? But I liked my own little world, small as it was, with me at the centre of it. I suppose you might think me selfish and you'd be right. As long as everything's going the way I want it, I'm happy. I'm a loner at heart. But not lonely. I know the difference. And if I wasn't exactly happy growing up, I was content in my own small way. So all that hard-earned money from my various small jobs – and I mean hard-earned in most cases – was unspent and I stashed it away, put it by for a nebulous event in the future. Which, as it happened, was quite handy because when I came to leave home I had enough for the deposit on the flat I currently rent. But I'm getting ahead of myself.

    Sixth form was coming to an end and I had no idea what I was going to do next. Army? No. I couldn't handle the discipline and I don't look good with a buzz cut. Apprentice? In what? Uni? Too expensive and I didn't relish a lifetime of debt. College? Same issues. I really was at a loss and, to be honest, although I wasn't starting to sweat about it, it was preying on my mind. I knew it was time to leave home – don't get me wrong, my parents are lovely people. Mum's a primary school teacher and Dad's something in roofing. Not sure what. I didn't give them any bother when I was growing up – no staying out all hours and coming home in the early hours of the morning reeking of cheap cider and vomit; no heavy metal played at full volume to annoy the neighbours; not the least interest even in the odd spliff – no, I was no bother to them at all. And they left me well alone to do whatever I wanted. Which, frankly, wasn't very much. In fact it does make me wonder exactly how I did spend my time growing up. What did I do with my youth? I'll have to ponder on that one.

And then I saw an ad in the local paper.

The town where I live, Lundby, used to be famous for its pottery, its wealth derived from particularly rich clay deposits found in the hills to the west. I know this because I went on a school trip once to see the only kiln left standing, all the other buildings connected with the pottery having been torn down or converted to over-priced (ie out of my price range) flats. The brownstone pots that were produced in their hundreds of thousands were popular for their functionality rather than their finesse (so we were informed), and as long as the clay lasted, so did the town's wealth. But, needless to say, the combination of the clay running out with the once-famous pots falling out of favour, caused Lundby to fall into the doldrums. With unemployment rampant – 1 in every 5 inhabitants had worked in the potteries – the town officials turned their attention to any means of attracting employers who could help regenerate yet another dying, unloved northern town. High tech was the answer they decided, and eye-watering amounts of money (mostly from the government) were invested in building a technology park on the outskirts. Huge glass and steel sheds soon became home to the latest in IT-based companies, mostly foreign of course, but, typically, I somehow found myself not only working for one of the few British companies, but based in a re-purposed cinema right in the centre of town.

When I first saw the ad in the paper I almost ignored it. "Bunged up? Got a blockage in your system?" it asked. "Logjams are our speciality!" I decided I did not want to work as a plumber or for a drains company. Fortunately I read on. "Bright young person required for a high pressure, high satisfaction role in a modern logistics company. Be part of our future and we'll be part of yours." A telephone number and email address followed.

To be honest, I'd never really given too much thought as to my future. Something would turn up, I was sure of that and I was happy to wait. For a wee while at least. But then I saw this and thought, what was there to lose? I called the number and had an interview the next day. The company, Free Flow-ers Logistics International, had its head office in the converted Ritz Movie Theatre in the heart of Lundby – not the high spec brand new office I'd have preferred but it turned out to be convenient. The building itself was not unattractive. Brick built with art-deco stained glass in every window, it towered over the adjacent shops and fast food outlets, lending an air of faded elegance and charm to an otherwise nondescript town centre. Decorative glazed tiles surrounded each of the three arches which graced the front of the building. In bygone days the central arch led into the foyer. Now it was the Reception and it was there I waited nervously, having told the receptionist my name and the time of my interview.

A young guy with a red and white striped goatee – Rufus, his name-badge announced – conducted the interview, such as it was. He didn't look very much older than me to be honest, and, in all the time I've worked here, I've never seen him since. He asked me if I saw the pun in the company name. Not Flowers, he said. Flow-ers. Geddit? Geddit? he demanded. Yes, I goddit. Hilarious! Notwithstanding the fact that I understood, he went on at great length to make sure that I fully appreciated that the company's purpose was nothing to do with flowers but was a logistical one – ensuring the safe and rapid distribution of goods nationally and worldwide, whether it be gravy granules from the factory to the supermarket or high-cost precision aero parts delivered to engineers who were waiting to fit them into broken aircraft. Although, he added, almost conspiratorially, sometimes flowers might actually be involved. I just nodded my head frequently. In fact, I can't remember saying very much at all. But what little I did say was obviously enough as I was offered a job on the spot. He told me it didn't pay well but promised there would be huge opportunities to advance and get promoted – and a bigger salary was always on the cards. It's not happened yet but it's early days, so I'm told, although I've been here close to 2 years now. To be frank, I'm not sure that even if I did earn shedloads more money I would change very much. I wouldn't move. I'm happy with what I've got. My life is ordered and that's what I like. Unexciting, you may say. I can't argue with that but that's fine by me. But you're only what? 19? 20? I hear you cry. You haven't even started to live your life yet! Maybe. Maybe not. But I'm okay with that too. You're sad, I can hear you whispering. Your words, not mine.

You'll spend most of your time on the computer, Rufus had told me. How did that sit with me? I told him it sat with me fine. (Frankly, I'm better with computers than I am with people. Not that I'm a geek, you understand. I just like my own company). And when could I start? Was tomorrow okay? I assured him it was. And that was that.

"Welcome to effin eff Logistics," he said, shaking my hand. At least that's what it sounded like.

Although Free Flow-ers is a large and growing company, I haven't progressed much beyond gravy granules yet, so to speak. I spend most of every day sitting in front of a computer looking after the supermarket distribution network for the North West and Scotland, which I suppose isn't bad considering the time I've been here, but it's less a reflection on my performance and more to do with the rapid turnover of staff. I could describe in detail what exactly I do but I know it would bore the pants off you. It sounds grander than it is but, trust me, it really is a small job. My Mum, bless her, thinks I do something very important but I don't. I'm just a small cog in a very large wheel. One day I may take on the world although I'm not sure whether North Africa is ready for Yummy Mummy Gusto Gravy just yet.

I suppose I could consider the day of my interview a big day in my life in as much as I'd started the morning unemployed and living at home and by the evening not only did I have a job but I had somewhere new to live. Because it was on the way home that I decided to call in at the nearest off-licence to buy a bottle of something fizzy so I could celebrate my good fortune with my parents. And the nearest off-licence was Ahmed's.

"You look cock-a-hoop," he said smiling. "Won the lottery?"

"Next best thing," I replied. "Got a job."

He seemed genuinely pleased for me.

"Need somewhere to live?"

I knew I wanted to have my own place but always thought it would be years down the line.

"I suppose so. Why?"

"Got just the place for you. Upstairs. Got 5 minutes?"

For a minute I thought I was being propositioned but, before I could answer, Ahmed had pushed me out onto the street, locked the shop door behind him and unlocked the door next to it. I followed him up a narrow flight of stairs. It took him fewer than 10 minutes to show me round the flat but I loved what I saw. Perfect.

"My cousin had it. Got a job in Canada now so won't be needing it any more. Needs a bit of a clean and a lick of paint but I could have it ready for you by next week. What do you say? Interested?"

I was. We agreed a not unreasonable rent and shook hands on it. And 10 days later I was in my new home.

So yes, all in all, that was definitely a big day for me. August 2nd. Worthy of at least two Shetland ponies! I always remember the dates of the big days, there are so few and that was one of the biggest to date. It's not every day you get a job and move into a new home at the tender age of 19! But mostly my days were small ones. Not that I was complaining, that's just the way my cookie crumbled.

※

You won't be surprised to know that I'm single. Not to say that I haven't had relationships. I have. It's just they've all been a bit on the small size, if you get my drift. Nothing earth-shattering, just a couple of fumbling teenage romances. Short and sweet. But I'm quite content. I have a couple of friends, Ahmed being one of them, and there's always my Mum and Dad and my sister, Becca. I'll tell you more about her later. So I'm not lonely. Far from it. And if I do keep every single one of my birthday and Christmas cards and put them out each and every year it's only because I'm big into recycling. Save the planet and all that stuff.

I'm not a virgin, though I'm as good as, these days. I lost my virginity at my first office Christmas party. If it ever came up in discussion, which of course it never would, I could always say that I was deflowered at the Ritz. It sounds better. But, in reality, it was all a bit grubby, and to say I'm not proud of myself is an understatement. My excuse? I was drunk at the time. Very. And worse, it was in the Stationary Cupboard, so named because neither it, nor anything in it ever moved. It was, in fact, not a cupboard but the old projectionists' booth which had been converted into a rather grandiose wash-room with an over-sized marble sink and a single cubicle. Where brown-coated men (always men) once loaded and unloaded films onto the projectors ensuring the smooth running of first black and white then colour movies, now floor-to-ceiling mirrors and harsh neon strip lights provided a different backdrop for a different purpose altogether. The Stationary Cupboard, despite being supposedly for the use of all members of staff, was only ever used by the floor manager, Ted, who could nearly always be found in there, sitting quietly, cigarette (banned) and porn magazine (proscribed) in hand, for hours on end. It was considered his domain and he rarely moved from it. If you had a query that was the first place to look.

Anyway, back to my first Christmas party. I hadn't planned on going initially. After nearly five months in the job I still didn't really know many people in the office. Because everyone sat glued to their computer day in day out and there wasn't much in the way of chatting and getting to know one's colleagues. And, as I said before, the turnover of the bright young things who were employed at Free Flow-ers was phenomenal – they always seemed to be moving on, boasting of something bigger and better – and much better paid, of course – so you never really got a chance to get to know anybody. We didn't have a uniform, thank goodness but we did have name badges. And believe me, without them I'd have been lost.

But the party. I thought it rude not to go. My first job. My first Christmas party. And who knew? I might finally get to talk to someone, someone interesting and fun. If not, I'd give it an hour then go home. But the party didn't turn out quite the way I'd hoped. It was something bigger altogether. And another first for me. One Shetland pony but for all the wrong reasons.

The top two floors of the building were open-plan offices accommodating some 50 odd staff and it was on the first floor where I worked that the festivities were to be held. The day had been hectic – some of my colleagues were trying to rearrange the desks in order to create a small dance floor whilst I was trying to deal with the aftermath of an overturned lorry on the M6 which had spilled its load of watermelons – there'd be a shortage in Birmingham unless I could find a replacement. Christmas is never the same without water melons, Ted told me. Other staff were standing on chairs, taping tinsel streamers and paper chains to the windows and hanging plastic Santas and reindeer from the ceiling lights. Loud Christmas songs belted out from a boom box on top of a cabinet and it was proving difficult to concentrate. Yet more colleagues had cleared a couple of desks of work paraphernalia and were emptying plastic carrier bags of what I understand is called party food. On a table in a corner, bottles of wine and cider, and cans of lager and beer competed with a few bottles of spirits and a large red bucket with 'Fruit Punch' written on the side in felt tip. I gave up on the lorry. It would be hours before the Police could sort it out and maybe some of the festive-coloured fruit could be salvaged. I looked up from my screen to find the room had suddenly become rammed with people, most of whom I'd never seen before. Standing up, I stretched my back and decided it was time to try and be sociable. I walked over to the food and helped myself to some miniscule pallid sausages and a few quarters of egg and cress sandwiches. Not seeing anyone I really wanted to talk to, not that conversation would have been remotely possible in that din, I went and got a plastic cup of the punch. I stood watching the chaos from the relative safety of the photocopier. I was amused to see that not only had the lid been firmly taped down but there was a note on it stating that under no circumstances was anyone to sit on this equipment or use if for anything other than its intended purpose. It was signed by one of the managers. What other purpose could there be? The punch was nice and fruity and seeing as it was the only non-alcoholic drink available, I refilled my cup. What I didn't know at the time was that some bright spark had fortified the bucket with several bottles of peach vodka. Peach vodka? I ask you! By the time I had enjoyed four cups, each one tasting better than the last, the room and everything in it seemed to have mellowed. I helped myself to another one.

"You're Rob, aren't you?" said a voice to my right. I turned. Next to me was a girl I'd seen in the office before, but then it would have been hard not to. Her bright pink hair hung in two long plaits and her face was a mass of piercings – eyebrows, nose, lips, ears. She held her hand out to me. I noticed it was covered in spider-web tattoos. In my somewhat stupefied state I curiously found all this quite attractive.

"Jazz."

"Pardon?"

It was difficult to hear her above the relentless throb of the music.

"Jazz. My name's Jazz," she shouted.

I shook her hand.

"I'm Rob," I bellowed.

"I know, numbnuts! I just said that."

I smiled at her.

"Enjoying the party?"

"What?"

"I said… Never mind! Want to go somewhere quieter where we can talk?"

I had no idea what she'd said so I just smiled and nodded. Jazz took me by the hand. And the rest, as they say, is history.

She pointed in the direction of the Stationary Cupboard, which to my mind was not living up to its name and I had to blink several times to get my eyes to focus. I tried to concentrate on Jazz as she weaved her way through the sweating, grinding bodies on the dance floor, and like a lamb to slaughter, I followed meekly. Once inside, she pushed the door shut with her foot and then pounced. There's no other word for it. All I could hear was the thump thump thump of the music in the next room which matched the rhythm in my head perfectly. Jazz's tongue, now down my throat, combined with the relentless clamour, only added to my increasing desire to throw up. If you ask me to describe what happened between us, I'm afraid you'll be disappointed. I'm not proud of what I did but Jazz clearly was.

"You're number 16," she said, licking my ear afterwards.

"16? I don't understand."

"You're the 16th I've shagged!"

I stared at her, open-mouthed.

"It's my hobby," she announced proudly.

Hobby? The need to upchuck was suddenly overwhelming. I yanked the Stationary Cupboard door open and stumbled into the throbbing Christmas festivities. With great difficulty I found the exit and, hanging on to the bannister like grim death, I staggered down two flights of stairs, through reception and out into the fresh air, where I promptly anointed the pavement with copious amounts of vomit. I continued in this vein all the way back to my flat where I fell into bed and slept for 12 hours.

When we were growing up my sister, Becca, was always on at me as to why I never had what she called a proper girlfriend. Where do you keep your hormones? she demanded. In a tin under the bed? She once asked me if I was gay. I'm not, but she said it wouldn't matter if I was; she'd still be my sister and nothing would change that. She told me that in the looks department, I was passable. I asked her, only half jokingly, what she meant. Did someone look at me then just pass on by? You'll do for someone one day, she insisted. Do what? I asked. And she'd smile at me, shaking her head. I don't think I'm anything special to look at – just short of 6 feet, skinny, with dark brown curly hair and deep-set eyes of the same colour. Baby-faced, I think. I tried to grow a beard once in an attempt to look more mature but I ended up with an unsightly itchy rash on my neck so I soon gave up on that. I mean, of course I had hormones. Still do. It's just that they're mostly quiescent.

You'd like Becca. I do. She's a generous soul. In reality we're chalk and cheese but we've always got on fine. Because of our age difference – Becca is seven years older than me – we didn't hang out together or anything like that when we were growing up but she was always my big sister and kept an eye out for me. As a youngster I spent most of my time in my bedroom, on the computer or reading; she was always out with her friends, spending every penny of her pocket money on clothes and make-up. And boys. My God! The rows she and our parents had when she came back late at night! Goody two-shoes that I was, I would be lying in bed, nose in a book, listening to them yelling at each other, my father insisting that she was grounded until she could show some evidence of common sense. It never happened – both my parents were way too soft. With her. And me. Then suddenly, overnight, all that changed and my sister became a new person. Becca had an epiphany. But it wasn't a religious one, thank God! No, my sister had decided she was going to become an actress.

The way it happened was this. In her last year in school, Becca developed an unexpected interest in the Drama Society. It shouldn't have been that unexpected – she fancied one of the boys involved and it was a way of getting close to him. She auditioned and, to her great surprise, was given the lead female role in the Christmas panto which was to be staged in front of all the pupils, teachers and as many parents who couldn't think of a sufficiently good excuse to get out of it. She played, to great acclaim, the wicked Mrs Cleaverage in Sweeney Plod, a deliciously macabre tale of a rookie PC, one Bayonet Butcher, (Nettie to his friends) who had his own misguided but unquestionably effective way of reducing crime on his patch. Becca's dark sultry looks were ideal for her sinister role as the policeman's occasional love interest. Anyway, to cut a long story short, her acting prowess was spotted by a parent in the audience who just happened to work for a small tv production company. He approached her afterwards, telling her she had the makings of a fine actress and, with his connections, could point her in the right direction. I reckon that was probably a three Shetland pony day for her. And although fame and fortune has, sadly, so far eluded her – she's had a couple of walk-on parts in a gritty, humourless soap opera based on the everyday life of mundane, unhappy folk with dire accents, she aspires to greater things. I'm keeping my fingers crossed for her, big style.

So there you have it. That's the story of me and my family – I've already told you about Mum and Dad. You can see now why I consider my life to be small and why I don't wake up every morning thinking "Is today the day?" I don't expect it to be and I'm pretty sure I don't want it to be. Today will be be like any other day – routine, tidy and just the way I like it. Obviously you'll think I'm an oddball since I'm not one of these people who covet what they haven't got. More money? More brains? Better job. Who doesn't want more? Everyone except me it would seem. What about your dreams? I hear you ask. Your aspirations? No, sorry. Haven't got either. Just happy the way I am. For now.

I never told Becca about the Christmas party incident – I never shared it with anyone until now. I was so ashamed of my behaviour. How could I have let myself be seduced by someone who regarded me as just another conquest? A slut with a score-sheet. I could have caught the clap or something worse. I should have got myself checked out but I didn't and after a few months, I stopped worrying about it. But I suppose it had put one demon to bed, so to speak. I had broken the duck. Fortunately my embarrassment was limited to me alone – Jazz, for whatever reason, failed to return to the office after the short Christmas break and everyone else who had been there was either too drunk or too stoned to notice, or care, about what had happened. So on the same day as a spillage of thousands of water melons on the motorway, I lost my single cherry in a very superior toilet. Not exactly something to tell the grandkids! What I can tell you is that the incident put me off alcohol forever and to this day, I can't come within sniffing distance of a peach without feeling the need to throw up. The same's not true for girls, it's just the opportunity isn't there at the moment.

None of this is terribly exciting. But life isn't, for most people. It's always the small things that make us happy and I'm no different. Or so I thought. But little did I know that my world was about to implode. Is that the best way to describe what happened? Probably not. But however I say it, I would never be the same person again. And if I'd known how my life was going to turn on its head would I have done anything differently? Dunno. All I know for certain is that my life, and everything I valued, changed once and for all. Bigly.

"Parcel for Rob James! Parcel for Rob James! Please collect from Reception."

Tannoy announcements in the office were few and far between and I'd certainly never been summonsed by one before. I glanced round. Everyone else was focusing on their computer. I checked my watch. Only half an hour to go until I packed it in for the day. I'd collect it on the way out.

"Parcel for Rob James! Immediate collection please!"

Just at that moment Ted chose to exit his salubrious sanctum. It was the first time he'd been seen all day. I watched him out of the corner of my eye as he wandered over in my direction. He stopped behind me and hissed in my ear.

"Don't approve of personal deliveries to the office," he said crossly.

"Sorry," I replied "I'm not expecting anything."

"Distracting. That's what it is."

I apologised again.

"Go on then. See what it is. We won't get any peace until you do."

I ran down the stairs two at a time.

"What's the hurry?" I asked the girl on Reception. Needless to say I didn't recognise her.

"Delivery driver said it needed to be collected immediately."

"Why? What is it?"

Sharleen, for that's what her name badge read, shrugged her shoulders and pointed to the very large cardboard box sitting on the counter. There were numerous holes on every side but nothing to identify what it was or who it was from. Or indeed, who it was for.

"I dunno what it is," she replied grumpily, "you tell me." She picked up her mobile and started scrolling.

"How did you know it was for me?"

"S'what the man said."

I picked up the box and shook it. It was surprisingly heavy but it made no sound.

"Who delivered it?" I asked her. "Which company?"

"I dunno." She didn't even look up.

"Are you sure it's for me? It's got no label on it."

Sharleen finally put her phone down and stared at me.

"Like I told you, the man said it was for you."

"Did he name me?"

"Of course he did. Else how would I know it was for you? I'm not thick, you know."

Really? But I said nothing.

I took the box back up to my desk. Opposite, Ryan looked up from his screen.

"Birthday present?"

"Not my birthday." I shook the box again. This time there was an unidentifiable sound from within. Like a snuffling.

"Are those air holes?" asked Ryan. "Could be a puppy."

"Only one way to find out."

Carefully I pulled off the parcel tape, opened the flaps and peered inside.

"Fucking hell!" I fell into my chair. I'm pretty sure this was the first time I'd ever sworn in my life. Properly sworn, I mean. But at least I had good cause.

"What is it?" asked Ryan.

I couldn't speak.

Ryan, intrigued, got up and came round to see what was in the box.

"Fucking hell!"

"What is it? What've you got?" asked several colleagues, attracted by the commotion.

"It's a bloody baby, that's what it is!" Ryan told them.

I closed the box. A baby?

"You can't do that!" cried Ryan. "It's got to breathe."

I opened the box again and had another look. By this time everyone in the office, including Ted, was crowded round my desk. There it lay, wrapped in a pink blanket, its small head crowned with sparse dark brown curly hair. Brilliant blue eyes looked up at me and it smiled gummily.

"Got your hair," said one of the girls leaning over to look inside the box.

"But I don't understand. I don't have a baby. I mean, not that I know of."

"Well you've got one now," said Ted, smirking.

"But I can't have. I mean I've never..."

"Well, you must have at some stage," laughed Ryan.

"That's not what I meant."

I felt sick. Surely this was a practical joke. Only it wasn't funny.

"Is there a note or something?" asked the girl. I read her name badge. Laura.

I carefully picked up the baby and held it at arms length whilst Laura rummaged round inside the box.

"Here," she said, passing me a white envelope with 'Rob' written in green ink on it, and swapping it for the baby. "Go on! Open it!"

There was a single word on the enclosed sheet of paper. 'Yours!'

Ted peered over my shoulder.

"Well, that clears that up then. No doubt about it!"

I turned the sheet of paper over and over, even sniffed it. There was a slight whiff of farmyards.

"It clears up nothing at all. Someone's having a laugh. Come on! Who is it? Which one of you is responsible?" I looked round the room.

"If that's a practical joke," said one of the men, "it sure as hell takes the biscuit!"

"He's right," said Ryan. "Who on earth would do something like this?"

The baby looked at me and gurgled.

"She's in a pink blanket," said Laura. "So that means she's a girl, right? You've got yourself a daughter."

"You could always double check," suggested Ryan.

I lay the baby on my desk and unfolded the blanket. Immediately an overpowering smell of something rotten and primeval caught the back of my throat. The group around me took a step back in unison.

"Phew! Do they always smell like that?"

"Smells like she needs changing," suggested Laura. "Here. Let's see if there's any nappies in the box."

Nappies? Suddenly my life contained nappies? And a baby, for that matter.

Laura found a small zipped bag from which she pulled out a couple of disposable nappies and a packet of wet wipes.

"Over to you," she said smiling.

"But I've never changed a nappy in my life," I cried. "I wouldn't know where to start!"

"Here," said an older woman. Mary. She must have been at least 40. "I'll show you."

Deftly she undid the poppers on the baby's all-in-one and opened up the nappy, revealing its contents. I gagged.

"Oh God!" whispered someone.

"Is that normal?" I asked looking at the baby as she smiled contentedly. "All that...stuff?"

"It's perfectly normal. She's a baby." Mary used half a dozen wet wipes to clean up the baby whilst we all watched in awe. "You're going to have to learn how to do this for your daughter. Because that's what she is. A little girl."

"Look," I said, imploringly, "I don't know that it is my daughter. She's been abandoned here and the only thing is that note that says 'Yours!' That doesn't prove she's mine."

"Nothing to say she isn't," smiled Ted. "And it's your name on the envelope!" He was loving every minute.

The baby started to cry.

"Needs feeding," suggested someone.

Everyone was an expert except me.

"And how do I do that?"

Mary looked at me.

"You really have no idea, do you?"

"No, I don't. I have absolutely no idea what to do with her."

Mary rocked the baby gently and put a knuckle in the baby's mouth. The child sucked greedily.

Suddenly I had an idea.

"Would you like her?" I asked.

"What? You can't just give away a baby!"

"Well, what else do I do with her? I have no idea how to look after her. I don't even know that she's mine. You look like you know what you're doing. You take her."

"Listen, Rob. I know what I'm doing because I raised 4 of my own. Isn't there someone who can give you a hand?" She gave me a long hard look. "The mother, for example?" Slowly a light bulb came on in my head.

"I'm not sure who the mother is," I said "I mean, I think I may know but I don't know that I'm the father."

The word sounded strange on my lips. Father?

"Sometimes you just have to take responsibility for your actions," Ted told me. "Be a man."

"I think it's being a man that's got him into this situation in the first place!" laughed Ryan.

There were nods all round.

"Look," I cried, begging. "Can't somebody help me? Please?"

"I tell you what I'll do," offered Mary. "If Ted lets us finish now I'll take you round to Boots and we'll get all the stuff you need for the baby for the next couple of days. How does that sound?" She looked at Ted who nodded.

"But what happens after that? What do I do then?"

"Well, I can only suggest that you try and contact the mother, or failing that, find someone who could look after the baby for you. Your Mother? Sister? A friend? And if you can't, it'll have to be Social Services."

"But I don't know about the mother," I whined. "If it is who I think it might be. Or where she is, if it is her." And who else could I ask? My mother? Becca? I didn't like the idea of ringing Social Services. That just didn't feel right somehow.

"Listen, if we're going to get to Boots before it closes, we'd better go now." Mary wrapped the baby back in her blanket and handed her to me.

"What you going to call her?" asked Ted.

Oh God! Something else I was going to have to do. Find a name for my alleged daughter. I'd never had so much excitement in my life and I wasn't sure I wanted it. This was turning out to be bigger than anything I'd ever dealt with before. As far as those Shetland ponies were concerned, today was off the scale.

The only free assistant in Boots was a stern-faced matron who was standing behind a counter on the front of which was a sign which read 'Family Planning'. Bit late for that I thought.

I explained to her that I needed a few bits and pieces for the baby.

"How old is it?" she asked frowning

I shook my head. "I don't know."

"You don't know?"

"I'm guessing about 6 months," said Mary helpfully. "We'll need everything a baby needs to tide us over for the next few days."

The Boots assistant eyed us both up and down. You could see her dying to ask. Are you the father? Are you old enough to have children? And is this the mother? Twice your age? Should I ring the police now or when you leave? I studied the shelves of condoms behind her very closely.

"We're going to need nappies, formula, a bottle, wipes, a couple of baby-grows and a bib," said Mary authoritatively.

The assistant sniffed loudly and started collecting the items.

"Formula? Why would we need a formula?" I asked.

"It's baby food, you moron!" she snapped. "You really are clueless, aren't you?"

I could only agree.

"Here we are," said the assistant putting a large carrier bag on the counter. "It's all in there."

I got out my credit card to pay.

"Bloody hell!" I swore again! "That's a lot of money!"

"Babies are very expensive things," said Mary. "That's why you should always think twice about having them."

The Boots woman could only nod vigorously in agreement.

I started to say something but decided against it. The baby was starting to fret. I rocked her gently in my arms, trying to soothe her.

"What's she called?"

Oh God! Not again! What was I going to call her?

Above the shelves of condoms was a startling advert – it featured a highly muscled man, naked from the waist up, with an impossibly self-satisfied grin on his face. 'Adonis Silky', I read. 'When your bit of rough needs something smooth'.

"Silkie!" I blurted out. "With an i e."

"Silkie?" asked the woman.

"Silkie?" asked Mary.

I nodded. "Pretty, isn't it?" It would have to do for the moment.

Mary picked up the bag and we left the shop.

"Where do you live?" she asked me.

"Just round the corner."

"I'll come back with you. Show you how to sterilise the feeding bottle, make up the feed and how to change a nappy. Then you're on your own."

"Thank you," I said, and boy, did I mean it!

An hour later Mary had gone leaving me with a clean and apparently contented baby. I'd sterilised the bottle with boiling water and, following the instructions on the packet, made up the correct strength of feed. Silkie had gulped it down. Mary had showed me how to burp her although this only resulted in a thin stream of white vomit down the back of my shirt.

"Perfectly normal," she'd reassured me. "It's what they do. Nothing to worry about. Now where is she going to sleep?"

"With me?" I suggested tentatively. "The bed's big enough."

"That's an absolute no-no!"

"The sofa?"

Mary looked at me as if I was an idiot.

"Have you got a chest of drawers?"

I nodded. "Up in the bedroom."

"Take one of the drawers out and put her in there."

"Really?"

"Really. It's what we used for our first 2 before we could afford a cot."

I was learning so much. Mary found her diary in her handbag and tore out a page. She wrote her mobile number on it and put it on the kitchen table.

"Only in a dire emergency," she warned.

I promised. She saw herself out and I sat down on the sofa, holding Silkie in my arms. She was gurgling away, clearly happy. I wiped dribble from the corner of her mouth with my shirt sleeve. How could something so little be so big? I couldn't take it in. She was beautiful. Tiny but colossal. And she was mine. Or so I'd been told.

Holding Silkie carefully I dialled my sister. Becca would be able to help me out. Take the baby off my hands until I got this sorted.

"Becca? Hi! How you doing?"

"Rob? Good to hear from you. You won't believe where I am!"

"Why? Where are you? Not in London?"

"No. I'm in Romania."

My heart sunk.

"Romania? What are you doing there?"

"I got this offer of a film part. Short notice. It's a Goth horror. Right up my street and it pays well. Couldn't say no. It might lead on to other stuff."

"Why didn't you tell me?"

"Sorry. No time. It was literally, drop everything and go. Hardly had time to throw a few things in a bag and get to Gatwick."

"Oh."

"You sound disappointed. Is everything okay?"

"Yes. No. I mean yes, everything's fine," I lied.

"I'm only away for another week then I'll be home. We can catch up then."

My heart sunk further. There'd be no help from my sister, then.

"You sure you're alright? You don't sound like your usual self."

Usual self? How could I be my usual self when suddenly there was a whole new aspect to me? Parenthood! My once organised, steady life with everything just the way I liked it, was suddenly and hugely out of kilter.

"I'm fine," I repeated.

"Listen, I've got to go. Me and the rest of the cast are going out for a drink. Gotta dash. Speak soon?"

She hung up as I nodded. Well, that went well.

As if in agreement Silkie farted loudly. The accompanying smell told me there was more to it than that. Could I leave things as they were or would I have to change her again? No, the stench was overpowering. I would be doing both of us a favour. Sighing heavily I took Silkie into the kitchen and did the necessary. The way we - we? - were getting through these nappies I'd have to buy some more tomorrow. I made myself a cup of coffee and took her back into the lounge. Who else could I ask for help? My mother? I didn't think so somehow. How could I explain to her that Silkie was the result of a one-night stand with a woman about whom I knew nothing? Except her name and that I'd been part of her very unusual hobby. There was also the issue that I'd been very, very drunk at the time. I could imagine the look of disappointment on my Mum's face. She and Dad had been quietly proud about me moving into a place of my own at my age – but Mum always said I had always been older than my years – 19 going on 40, she'd said the day I moved out. But she knew I'd been ready for my independence for a long time. And now look what I'd gone and done with it! No, I couldn't show her that I'd failed. But didn't all mothers want to be grandmothers? She'd never once hinted that she wanted grandchildren, either to me or Becca. Maybe I could introduce the idea gradually and then surprise her one day? Look Mum! Meet Silkie. Your granddaughter. Sorry I've not mentioned her before. No. Not a good idea. So that only left me with two options as far as I could see until Becca got home. Look after Silkie myself or track down Jazz and hand her back. I knew that neither would be easy. If Jazz had wanted to keep Silkie she wouldn't have had her delivered to me in a cardboard box. I guessed she probably didn't want to be found. But nothing was going to happen tonight so the best thing to do was sleep on it.

I took Silkie upstairs and removed the top drawer from the chest of drawers and put it on the bed. Making a nest for her amongst my underwear, I covered her with several hand towels. That should keep her warm. Bending down I kissed her gently on the forehead. She was already sound asleep.

༄

Silkie may have had a good night's sleep but that's more than could be said for me. My mind was in overdrive. How had I ended up in this situation? A 19 year old man with a baby? I mean, technically I was still a teenager. What were the chances of me becoming a father after my first and, so far, only proper sexual encounter? Was that normal? And bearing in mind this was my first real sexual experience, it did mean that if it was anyone's baby, it could only be Jazz's. But what had she meant when she said I was number 16? That night? In the office? Since last Thursday? And if I was the 16th, how did she know the baby was mine? Surely it could just as easily have been fathered by one of the other men she'd entertained? True, Silkie had dark curly hair but so do lots of people. I needed to talk to Jazz. For lots of reasons. But how could I find her? And what if I did succeed in finding her and she didn't want the baby back? And what if I couldn't track her down? How would I explain my daughter to my parents? Or what if I decided to keep Silkie then 10 years down the line Jazz suddenly appeared on the doorstep wanting her back? No, that wasn't going to happen. I couldn't keep her. I mean, how would I manage my job as well as looking after a baby? I couldn't. And quite simply, the bottom line was, did I really want a baby? At my age? No, I decided, there was no room in my life for a child. Silkie would have to go. But where? And to whom? I lay in silence in the dark, hardly daring to breathe, afraid to move lest I wake her. But she snuffled quietly, completely undisturbed by my increasingly desperate unanswered questions. Finally, through sheer exhaustion, I fell asleep, dreaming of armies of baby bootees marching through piles of steaming Sheltand pony poo.

The double whammy of Silkie bawling at the top of her voice and the smell woke me. Oh no! I thought. Again? How can such a tiny thing produce such copious amounts of that? And why did it have to stink so bad? I looked at my watch. Seven o'clock. At least she'd slept through the night, bless her. I lifted Silkie out of the drawer and placed her on my chest. She stopped crying straight away and lay there contentedly, gripping my thumb tightly in her tiny fist, whilst sucking noisily on the other.

"Hungry?" I asked her. "Come on, little one. Time to sort you out."

I filled the kitchen sink with luke-warm water and squirted in some washing up liquid. Carefully removing her babygrow and the very full nappy I sat her in the water. Immediately she started to laugh, thrashing her feet and splashing the water with her hands. In no time I was soaked. We played until the water cooled then I dried her off, put her in a fresh nappy and a new babygrow – this one was yellow with smiling cats. I made up some more formula, fed her, and put her back in the drawer whilst I got ready for work. During the night I'd decided that I'd take her into the office today – what choice did I have? Even if Ted kicked up a fuss, he'd see I had no option.

As it happened he was fine with it. I'd put Silkie in the bottom of a holdall lined with more towels and placed her next to my desk on the floor, the bag unzipped. Her gurgling soon announced her presence to my colleagues nearby. The girls in particular made more visits to the Ladies and the coffee station than usual, each time stopping off to peer into the bag and coo at Silkie. She thrived on the attention. I managed to feed and change her between dealing with whatever delivery crisis arose – fortunately nothing major – and mid-morning I asked Ryan to keep an eye on her.

"Me?" he squealed. "Why me?"

"Because you're nearest."

"Where are you going?"

"Down to HR. I'm going to try and track down the baby's mother."

"So you know who it is?"

"I'm pretty sure."

"Don't be too long, will you?"

"Any problems ask Mary. She knows everything there is to know about babies."

HR was situated on the ground floor behind Reception. It was in the old cinema manager's office. I'd never been in the room before and as I knocked on the door, I tried to envisage a cigar-smoking be-suited man with slicked back hair sitting at a leather-topped desk counting the day's takings. Instead I got Malory. True, she was sitting behind a desk but this was more flat-pack than burnished oak. Ranks of grey steel filing cabinets stood to attention behind her. The only other item of furniture was a folding metal chair opposite her. Malory pointed to it and I sat down.

"What?" she demanded. She was clearly not one of the bright young things in the office. At a guess she looked to be about as old as the building but less well preserved.

"I'm after some information," I told her.

"I don't do information. I'm HR."

"I know you are. That's why I'm here."

Malory's nose whistled as she exhaled.

"What do you want then? I haven't got all day."

The open magazine in front of her said otherwise.

"I'm trying to find out the address of someone who used to work here."

"Why?"

"Well, it's rather delicate." I squirmed uneasily in my seat.

"Why?"

"Why what? Why is it delicate?" I asked.

She stared at me, lips pursed.

"I can't just give out information willy nilly, you know." She folded her arms across her flat chest.

"I know that," I said, trying to sound reasonable, "but I do have a really good reason for wanting to find someone. I need to talk to them."

"What about?"

"Like I said, it's delicate. Personal." This was proving to be far from easy.

"Hmmm."

"Hmmm, what?"

Malory leaned forward, squinting.

"It's like this, Ron,"

"Rob," I corrected her.

"It's like this, Rob. I can't help you unless you help me. You need to tell me who you want to find and why. I'm assuming that since you've come to HR the person doesn't work here any more."

I've already told you that, numpty!

"Spot on!" I cried. "You've nailed it in one!" Maybe a bit of flattery would help. Looking at her, I doubt anyone had ever flattered her before! "Absolutely. You're so right! Well done!" Steady, don't overdo it.

"And who might this person be?"

"Jazz."

"Jazz? What sort of name is that?"

"Hers," I replied. "It was her name."

"First or second?"

I looked at her blankly.

"First name or second name?"

"Oh. First."

"And her second name?"

"I don't know."

"Then I can't help you. We file everything under the surname. No surname, no can help."

I looked at my watch, mindful of the fact that I'd been away from my desk for a long time but more importantly, away from Silkie. Was she fretting without me? Was Ryan taking good care of her. Did she need feeding? Changing?

"Look, Malory, can I lay my cards on the table? This is all a bit embarrassing. Can I trust you?"

"Trust me?" The woman was truly indignant. "I'm HR here at Free Flow-ers Logistics. Discretion is my middle name. I didn't get where I am today without being able to hold my tongue."

Okay, I thought. Here goes. "I need to get in touch with Jazz to talk to her. She's left her baby with me and I ..."

"So you're the baby man! Everyone's talking about you! The whole office! No good'll come of it, I told Sharleen yesterday."

I stood up, fuming.

"Thanks for nothing," I said sarcastically. "You've been a big help."

Malory shrugged her shoulders.

"I couldn't give you her address anyway. Company policy, I'm afraid."

I slammed the door behind me.

⁂

"Where the hell have you been?" hissed Ryan. "Ted's been doing his nut!"

"Sorry. How's Silkie?"

I looked into the holdall. She was fast asleep, bless her. I straightened the towels.

"Oh, she's fine. Ask me how I am!"

"How are you, Ryan?"

"Stressed. You cannot leave me with a baby, man!"

"Why not? Somebody did it to me!"

"How d'you get on with Malory Glowers? Find what you were looking for?"

I shook my head.

"That's one formidable woman," I said.

"Woman? That's a bit generous!"

"She's happy to discuss my predicament with everyone else in the office but won't give me an inch."

"So what next?"

"See if I can track down the delivery company. They must have all the details of who placed the order. The fact that the man named me specifically means they must have some sort of record."

"Who was on Reception yesterday?"

"Sharleen."

"You do pick 'em, don't you! Good luck."

"It's all I've got to go on. Not unless you know if Jazz had any friends in the office."

"Jazz? Is that who's the mother?" Ryan looked pale.

"Yes. It couldn't be anyone else. Why?"

"Well, it's not so much a case of did she have any friends in the office, it's more the sort of friends she had, if you get my drift."

"Only too clearly, unfortunately."

I suddenly had a bad thought.

"You weren't one of those friends, were you, Ryan?" I could be looking at Silkie's father.

"No, mate. Not me. Got a girlfriend. She'd cut off my nuts if she thought I was cheating on her."

I was relieved. I liked Ryan but didn't like the idea of him being Silkie's dad. But that still left all the other men in the office. Including Ted? I couldn't go round all the men in F'n'F asking them if they'd slept with Jazz. So unless she had a particular friend, maybe a girlfriend, in whom she'd confided, all I had to go on was Sharleen.

"Listen. Can you cover for me for 10 minutes or so?"

"Where are you going now?"

"Sharleen."

"Not now, you're not." Ryan, nodding towards the Stationary Cupboard from which Ted was emerging, his face like thunder.

"Rob! My office! Now!"

"Good luck," whispered Ryan.

I'd only been in Ted's office on a few occasions, probably as many times as the man himself. I could see why he preferred the Cupboard. I closed the door to the cramped dark room behind me and wiped the dust from a chair before I sat on it.

"Now look, Rob. I'm a patient man. And I love kids. I've got three grandkids of my own, I'll have you know. But I don't bring them to work and I can't have you doing that either."

"Yes, I know, and I'm sorry, Ted. But at the moment I've got no choice. There's no-one else to look after her."

"Well then, you're going to have to find someone. And soon! She's distracting the whole office. Most of the girls can't take their eyes off her; some of the men too. And you've been away from your desk most of the morning."

"I'm trying to find the baby's mother. Get her to take her back."

"That's as maybe but Ryan had to deal with a cock-up in Kilmarnock whilst you were away. A lorry load of Spanish tomatoes was delivered to a bicycle repair shop instead. And the tyres the repair shop were expecting went to a hospital maternity unit. Our reputation's at stake. You should have been here."

"I am really sorry Ted. But I need to sort this out."

Ted leaned back in his chair and folded his arms.

"Look. I'm not an unreasonable man. You're a good worker and I'd hate to lose you."

The threat was left hanging. I thought it best to say nothing.

"How much time do you need?"

I thought quickly. If the delivery company could give me an address for Jazz I could sort this out quickly and return the baby to her. If not, then I had no option but to get my mother to help out and to live with the embarrassment and humiliation.

"A couple of days max."

"Two days, Rob. And you'll take it out of your annual leave."

"Thanks Ted. I really do appreciate it."

One way or another there had to be a solution and I now had 2 days in which to find it. I stood up to go.

"Oh and Rob? You'll need to go out in your lunch break to get some more nappies. We used the last one an hour ago."

I smiled broadly as I returned to my desk.

Sharleen was still scrolling on her phone in Reception when I got back from Boots weighed down with several bags containing nappies, formula and several soft toys.

"Hi," I said.

"Hi back."

"Remember me?" I asked her. "From yesterday?"

"Oh yes. I remember you," she sniggered.

"Can you remember the name of the delivery company? The one that left the cardboard box for me?"

"The one with the baby in it?" She smirked. "How could I forget? It's not like everyday someone drops off a baby for collection. It must have been StorksRUs!" She laughed uproariously.

"Very funny. I'm serious."

Sharleen shrugged her shoulders.

"I don't recall."

"But don't you have to sign for deliveries?"

"In theory."

"In theory?"

"Sometimes I forget. Yesterday was one of those times."

I could not believe what I was hearing.

"But there was no label on the box. Nothing to say who it was from or who it was for. But you said the delivery man said it was for me."

"That's right. He did."

"Do you remember what he was wearing?"

"Who?"

"The delivery man. Did he have a uniform on?"

Sharleen thought hard.

"And?" I prompted.

"Sshh. I'm thinking."

How long would it take? I wondered.

"Naa. He didn't have a uniform. It was just, like, jeans and a hoodie."

What sort of delivery company ran a business which didn't advertise itself? No identification on the box or the delivery man himself.

"What about a van? Did you see his van?"

Sharleen nodded.

"White, it was." She smiled, pleased with herself for having remembered something which might be useful.

"Did it have any logo on the side?"

"Any what?"

This was like teaching tadpoles to dance.

"A logo. You know, a brand name. Something which would identify the company."

Sharleen shook her head slowly.

"Nope. Nothing like that. I think I'd remember."

Somehow I doubted it.

Suddenly her face lit up.

"What?"

"CCTV!" she announced proudly. She nodded to a wall-mounted camera just above her head. A red light winked at me. "It's, like, for safety and stuff. So we can keep a record of what's going on. Who comes into the building. That sort of thing."

"Really?" Hope at last.

"Except..."

My heart sunk again.

"Except what?" I asked. I knew her answer would not be good.

"I remember now. I took the tape out a couple of days ago and forgot to replace it. There's no tape in there." She bit her bottom lip.

"So you're telling me that somebody dropped off a baby here yesterday, said it was for me, and we have no way of finding out which delivery company it was, and, consequently, who paid for

the delivery to take place?" I was trying to remain calm but it was becoming increasingly difficult.
"Consequ..what?" Sharleen sniffed.
"You won't tell on me, will you? For forgetting to put a new tape in?"
"Tell on you? I'd like to fucking kill you!"
She burst into tears.
I left her to it. This had been my last chance at finding out who had arranged for the baby to be delivered to me. Without details of the delivery company I wouldn't be able to track down Jazz. Which meant I couldn't return Silkie to her mother. I was stuck with her.

Before I left the office for the day I pinned a note to the notice board in the tea station. I was out of ideas on how to track down Silkie's mother and this was the last thing I could think of doing.
Help! Does anyone know how I can get in touch with Jazz? Please!
I included my name and phone number.
Everyone in the office knew why I was asking. Maybe someone knew where she was and would take pity on me. All I could do was hope. Ryan was going to have to look after my workload for the next two days so I gave him a brief run-down on what was in the pipeline. He wasn't too happy about it, needless to say. I owed him one – and Ted – big style.
Somewhat reluctantly I left work and headed home. At least in the office I was surrounded by people who could help me out with Silkie, even if most of them didn't know what they were doing. And then there was always Mary, who did. Until I got my Mum

involved, it was just going to be the two of us, Silkie and me. I'd ring my mother tonight and ask her to come over. Then my baby would be off my hands. Funny how I was starting to think of her as my baby when there was still no absolute proof that she was.

Silkie grizzled loudly as I unlocked the door to my flat and the holdall rocked violently. Time for a feed and a change. Again. I was getting used to recognising the signs. Suddenly Ahmed appeared at my shoulder.

"Alright?" he asked.

"Fine."

Silkie started to whimper.

"You know I don't allow pets in the flat, don't you?"

"Pets?"

"Yes, Rob. Pets."

"Why d'you ask?" I was perplexed.

"The wife said she heard a noise this morning. Said it sounded like a dog yowling. There's a no pet policy. Remember? Mucky things, especially when they're not toilet trained."

"I haven't got a pet," I told him, laughing, "but what I have got is definitely not toilet trained."

Ahmed looked worried as the bag moved again.

"What's in there then?"

I bent down and lifted Silkie out. An unpleasant smell accompanied her. Ahmed took her from my arms and looked at her adoringly.

"Is she yours?"

"I don't really know," I answered. "She might be. I think so."

"What sort of answer's that?"

"It's the best I can do at the moment," I said. "I'm trying to find out one or two things."

"Well you're a dark horse, ain't ya? I never would have suspected."

He laid her against his shoulder and gently patted her back. Silkie gurgled happily.

"No dog then?"

"No. No dog. Just a baby."

"Who'd have thought it? You of all people!"

"What do you mean?" I asked indignantly. "Why shouldn't I have fathered a child?"

"Well, you being so quiet an' all. Never heard a peep out of you all the time you've been living here and now look at you. A Dad! I'd never 'ave believed it!"

Ahmed grimaced in disgust.

"Phew! Needs changing."

"I know. And feeding. If it's not one, it's the other."

"Come into the shop. Let me show her to the missus."

I relocked my front door and followed Ahmed into the off-licence and through a door into a back office. The room was stacked with boxes and crates from floor to ceiling – crisps, chocolate, bottled water, beer, spirits of every description – you name it, it was there. In the middle was a table at which sat a middle-aged woman dressed in a salwar kameez totally engrossed in what she was doing on a lap top. She glanced up at me as I walked in and nodded.

"Rob. This is me wife. Ayesha."

I smiled but the woman was no longer looking at me.

"What's that?" she squealed, pointing. "A baby? Gimme! Gimme!"

Ahmed passed Silkie to her and immediately she started cooing – there was no other word for it.

"Where d'ya find this little darling?" she asked, stroking Silkie's cheek. "Bubububub."

"She's Rob's. Rob. Our tenant from upstairs."

Finally Ayesha looked at me.

"Yours?"
I nodded.
Ahmed patted me on the back.
"I knew she'd want to see it. Loves babies, does the wife."
"What's her name?" asked Ayesha. "I'm presuming it is a she?"
"Silkie. With an i e"
"Very pretty. But someone needs changing. Pooh! Stinky bum!"
I assumed Ahmed's wife was referring to Silkie.
"Can I change her? Can I?"
"Do you want to?" I asked.
Ayesha nodded vigorously. "More than anything."
Women were strange things.
"Have you got a spare nappy in there?" Ayesha nodded towards the holdall.
I had. No sooner had I got one out of the packet than she'd whipped off the dirty one and replaced it.
"There you go, good as new." She beamed at me. As did Silkie.
"Would you like her?" I blurted out.
"What?"
Now why on earth did I say that? Clearly the woman was obviously completely enamoured with Silkie and clearly knew what she was doing. She'd be ideal to look after my baby. But did I really mean what I'd just said?
"I mean...I can't keep her."
"Then why d'you have her?" asked Ahmed.
"Good question," I replied.
"Are you serious?" asked Ayesha, in total disbelief. "You would give her to me? You'd let me keep her?"
"Hang on a minute," said her husband. "One, Rob, you can't just go round giving your baby away. And two, Ayesha, no!"
"Oh please," she begged, tears in her eyes. "You know how much I want a baby."

Gently Ahmed took the baby from her and passed her back to me.

"Here. Take her. She's yours. Now go!"

Ayesha was weeping loudly, head in her hands.

"I'll be upstairs in 10 minutes if I may?" he asked, ushering me towards the door. I left quietly. What had I done?

"What were you thinking of?" Ahmed demanded. "Upsetting my wife like that?"

I was sitting at the kitchen table feeding my daughter. My left arm had gone to sleep so I switched Silkie to the other side. Her bottle was almost empty.

"I'm sorry. I didn't think. It's just she looked so happy with Silkie. So natural."

"We can't have kids. Me and her. It's all she ever wanted." Ahmed wiped his eyes. "Me too, if you want to know."

"I had no idea. I really am so very sorry."

"Why do you want to give her away? You know you can't do that, don't you? You'll have Social Services and the Police after you."

"The thing is I don't want to give her away. Not really. But I can't keep her."

I passed Silkie to Ahmed while I made him a cup of tea and told him the whole sorry tale, omitting the detail about me being number 16 on the score sheet. I'd envisaged spending the evening telling this story – also an amended version – to my mother and here I was recounting it to my landlord. He shook his head in disbelief.

"So you don't even know if she's yours."

"No. But in a way, I'd like her to be."

"Then why offer to give her away?"

"Panic. And it's not the first time," I admitted guiltily. "I offered her to a woman in the office yesterday. She knew what she was doing with Silkie as well. As it turned out she already had four of her own. I wouldn't have thought one more would have made any difference."

"What did she say?"

"Said her husband wouldn't agree."

"Thank goodness someone's got some sense. Because you sure don't have!"

Ahmed was right. I wasn't handling this well at all. Offering my baby to two strangers.

"And you decided to offer the baby to my wife because the other woman wouldn't take it?"

"No. It wasn't like that. I just did it on the spur of the moment, without thinking. Again! Honest. Ayesha just looked such a natural with Silkie. I had no idea of the pain I would cause. I wouldn't have hurt her for anything. I really am so very sorry."

"You saw her reaction? She'd have taken the baby in a second if I'd let her."

I hung my head in shame. What more could I say?

"But what I don't understand, Rob, is why you can't keep her. If you really do wish she was yours, what's the problem?"

"I'm not even 20 yet. I'm too young to have a baby."

"Not too young to father one."

"If she is mine. Which she may not be. I don't know."

"But what if she is yours? Why not keep her?"

"I've got my job. I can't look after a baby as well as work." I couldn't tell him that was only part of the reason. How could he understand that my life was just the way I wanted it. Ordered. With no room for any disruption in it. Certainly no room for a baby. "It's selfish, I know. Here I am with a baby I don't know if I want, and there's you and Ayesha, wanting desperately what you can't have. I feel awful."

"And so you should," admonished Ahmed. "Fatherhood is a blessing. You don't know how lucky you are." He stood up and put his hand on my shoulder. "You need to man up. Take responsibility for your actions."

If indeed they were my actions. I gazed down at Silkie, fast asleep in my arms.

"She's a gift. Never forget that," Ahmed said quietly.

And he left.

Ahmed was right. Silkie was a gift. How could I have ever thought otherwise? What sort of person was I to offer her to two strangers? First Mary then Ayesha. I didn't know either of them yet I had asked them both if they wanted to take my daughter. Poor Ayesha would have bitten my hand off. But what was I thinking? And what Ahmed had said was so true. You don't just give your baby away. Apart from the fact it was certainly highly illegal you'd have to be heartless to do so. Inhumane. I was ashamed of myself on so many fronts. How could I have succumbed to the questionable charms of such an evil person as Jazz in the first place? That answer was easy. I'd been drunk at the time. But even more to the point, how could I then offer to give my baby away? My daughter. But then wasn't that exactly what Jazz had gone and done? Given her baby away to a virtual stranger? I mean, apart from the fact that I was probably the father of her child, she hardly knew me. What sort of mother would give her child away to someone she'd slept with once? And what sort of person was she in the first place to brag about her hobby, keeping a tally of the number of men she'd slept with? Awful, awful woman. Silkie wriggled against me and let out a tiny sigh. No, I'd made my mind up. I didn't want to find Jazz and I was going to stop looking immediately. I couldn't hand Silkie back to someone like that. If Jazz could give her baby away apparently without a second thought then I didn't want her to be part of my daughter's life. I'd keep Silkie however hard it was going to be. Mum would come to love her. Dad too. They'd make wonderful grandparents. And Becca? Of course my sister would love her too. How could she not? Okay, I might still not be 20 yet, convinced that my life was the way I wanted it, but who was to say that couldn't change? Sure, the baby's arrival had been unexpected but maybe it would be the making of me. I could be a good father and I would love my daughter.

I propped Silkie up between two cushions and turned on the tv whilst I made myself some toast. The two of us had settled down to watch a documentary about the benefits of eating chocolate when the front doorbell rang. Ahmed coming back to remind me what a bad person I was? I looked forward to telling him I'd changed. I was a new man with a daughter to raise. But it wasn't Ahmed.

"Hello," she said quietly. "Are you Rob?"

I nodded.

"Can I come in and see my niece?"

I stared, open-mouthed, at the woman. Girl.

"Your niece?" I struggled to get the words out. My mind was in overdrive.

"Misty. My niece."

I shook my head vigorously.

"No-one here by that name." I started to close the door.

"Please. Jasmine was my sister. Jazz."

I looked harder. Yes there was a slight resemblance but this girl was softer, plumper, with no piercings, at least that I could see. She was shorter than me and her long black hair was tucked behind her ears. But if this was Silkie's aunt maybe she'd come to take her away from me? Perhaps she had some sort of claim on her. I couldn't let that happen.

"No, sorry. You've made a mistake," I insisted.

"But you are Rob, aren't you? From Free Flow-ers?"

I could hardly deny it.

"I am. But there's no Misty here. Nobody here by that name."

"Please. My name's Poppy. I'd just like to see Misty. That's all. See my sister's baby."

"No," I insisted, "there's no baby here."

Just at that moment there was a thud from upstairs followed by a long wail. Oh God! Silkie had fallen off the sofa! I ran up the stairs, Poppy close on my heels.

Silkie lay on the floor, screaming her head off. I picked her up, frantically searching for any broken bones or bleeding. Not finding any signs of damage, I rocked her gently, shushing her and she soon stopped crying. I gave her one of the soft toys I'd bought. It looked like an alien bunny on steroids, bright green with bulbous eyes. She loved it.

"Looks like you're a natural," said Poppy.

"Look, what do you want?" I asked her sharply.

"I just wanted to see Misty, that's all."

"Why? She's mine. And she's called Silkie. Not Misty. Jazz, your sister, she gave her to me."

"I know. She said she would."

Poppy looked longingly at the baby.

"She told you what she was planning to do?" I asked her.

Poppy nodded.

"Well I'm glad someone knew what was going on. Because I was completely in the dark. The first I knew of Silkie was two days ago when..."

How could I put this delicately? I couldn't.

"My daughter was delivered to me in a cardboard box at work with a single note. It read 'Yours!' That's all it said."

I was amazed to see Poppy smile.

"Typical Jazz!"

"You seem to know an awful lot so you'll probably already know that Jazz and I had what can only be described as a fling at the office Christmas party. That would be over, let me see, 15 months ago. I'm not proud of it but it seemed the norm for her. In fact, she told me I was the 16th man she'd slept with. I didn't know whether she meant that day, that month, ever!"

"Slept with 16 men?" Poppy sounded incredulous. "I doubt it. Jazz always did tend to exaggerate things. And if she said she'd slept with that many people you can bet your bottom dollar most of them would have been women!"

"What do you mean?"

"What do you think I mean? Jazz would sleep with anyone who took her fancy. Of either sex. But she preferred the ladies."

"Oh." There was clearly a great deal more to Jazz than I ever could have imagined.

"Please. Can I hold her?"

Silkie wriggled restlessly against me, grizzling.

Reluctantly I passed her to Poppy and turned the tv off. I headed into the kitchen.

"Tea?"

Poppy nodded and sat down on the sofa.

"I've not seen anything of Jazz since that night," I continued. "She never came back to work. She's never been in touch. I never knew about our baby until days ago, as I said. It came as a bit of a shock to find out I was a father. The father. Although I've still not seen any proof that I am. I still don't know if it might not have been one of the other men she slept with."

"She looks the spit of you."

"That's not evidence."

"Jazz told me she had the hots for someone at work. Someone she really liked the look of. Described you to a T."

"Really? She fancied me? She never said anything. Just pounced. I thought I was a one-night stand. Or not even that long."

I made two mugs of tea and carried one over to her.

"Have you eaten?"

Poppy shook her head.

"I was just going to have some toast. Want some?"

"That would be nice. If you don't mind."

"How did you find me?" I asked her.

"Your note. At work. I used to date one of the guys at FFL. He knew Jazz and I were sisters. He rang me to tell me you were looking for her. It wasn't difficult. Did you try to find Jazz? Once you'd got Misty, Silkie, I mean."

She bounced the baby on her knee. Silkie beamed toothlessly.

"Why did you call her Silkie, by the way?"

I didn't like to tell Poppy her niece was named after a condom.

"Jazz never told me her name. It just seemed to suit her."

"It does. It's pretty."

Poppy tickled Silkie who chortled in delight.

"So you're going to keep her?"

"That's the plan."

"Wow! That's amazing. I mean, a couple of days ago you didn't know you had a baby and now you're proposing a lifetime's commitment. That's going some!"

"And I intend to be a good father," I said, trying to sound convincing.

"I'm sure you do. Respect!"

I watched Poppy play with her niece. Something she'd said resurfaced.

"You said Jazz was your sister?"

"You don't know, do you?"

"Know what?" I demanded.

"Jazz died yesterday."

Poppy promptly burst into tears and Silkie, frightened by the unexpected noise, followed suit.

I sat down next to Poppy, not knowing what to say. I couldn't work out how I felt. The mother of my daughter was dead but it wasn't as if I'd ever known her. I took Silkie from her and gently rubbed her tummy. It seemed to soothe her and she stopped crying and promptly fell asleep.

"I'm sorry," was the best I could do.

Poppy sniffed loudly.

"You really didn't know?"

"How could I? As I said, she was never in touch. I saw her at the party and that was it. She never came back to work."

"It's such a shame," said Poppy. "I think you'd have been good for her."

I didn't know what to say to that.

"Were you close to your sister?" I asked.

The question caused Poppy to start crying again.

"Some. But she was a difficult person."

"I'd worked that out for myself these last few days," I said ruefully.

"She wasn't all bad, you know. She was a good mother. But she had her problems."

"I'd like to know about her, if you can bear to tell me. After all, she was Silkie's mother."

"Can I have another cup of tea?" she asked.

I obliged.

"Do you know why Jazz never returned to work after Christmas?" Poppy asked me.

I shrugged my shoulders.

"I just assumed she'd found something bigger and better, in every respect – the job and me. Few people seem to stay long at FFL so I just thought she'd gone to work somewhere else. And because I never imagined for one minute that I meant anything to her, other than a festive quickie, I never gave it a second thought. In fact, in a way, I was relieved she didn't come back. Saved me a lot of embarrassment. I don't go around doing that sort of thing."

Poppy didn't need to know it was my first time.

"You're very honest, aren't you?" She sipped her tea. "You didn't know that Jazz was ill?"

I shook my head.

"We'd had a lovely family Christmas together, our parents, our two brothers, Simon and Alfie. Then the day after Boxing Day she rang to tell us she had really bad stomach pains and didn't feel at all well. I joked that she'd had too many mince pies but she said she felt so awful, she was going to take a taxi to A&E. I said I'd meet her there. To cut a long story short, they did a whole raft of tests and told her they thought it was serious. It might be cancer. Stomach cancer. Some Christmas eh? Anyway, the hospital scheduled an urgent appointment with a specialist and sent her home."

Poppy blew her nose loudly, waking Silkie abruptly.

"Sshh. Go back to sleep, little one."

The baby did as she was told.

"I went with Jazz about a month later to see the oncologist. He did a whole load more tests and then told her the original diagnosis was correct and not only that, but she may have had it for a long time."

"I'm so sorry," I said. "I can't imagine how hard it must have been for you both. And the rest of your family."

Poppy sighed deeply before she continued.

"Before we left, the specialist asked if there was any way Jazz could be pregnant. When she asked him why he told her that the treatment was pretty unpleasant and might possibly harm a foetus. I remember Jazz grabbed my hand so tight it hurt. She stood up and looked at him long and hard. 'If I am pregnant,' she told him, 'there is no way you're going to harm my baby.' He tried to reason with her but she was having none of it. He tried to reason with me. I promised to do what I could but, knowing my sister, I'd be wasting my breath. On the way home we bought a pregnancy testing kit. Guess what?"

"Silkie."

"Silkie." Poppy dried her eyes before continuing. "Jazz moved back in with our parents. They did everything under the sun to try and persuade her to have the chemo and the radiotherapy and all that stuff but she wouldn't change her mind. Her baby was more important to her than life itself."

A tear rolled down my face. I'd had no idea at all. Silkie's mother had chosen to have her rather than undergo life-saving or at least life-lengthening treatment. I could hardly look at Poppy.

"Funnily enough, Jazz thrived throughout the entire pregnancy. She positively glowed and went round with her hands cupping her stomach, even when she hardly showed. It's funny. She'd always been a bit of a rebel, growing up. But motherhood changed her. She was a different person. Fortunately the stomach pains disappeared for a while and you'd never have known how seriously ill she was. Of course we all spoiled her – whatever she wanted she had. She had to have a Caesarian as they thought she was too weak for a natural birth. Jazz argued long and hard but finally gave in. We all tried to persuade her to have the treatment after she'd had Misty, arguing that it could give her more time with her daughter. But she wouldn't. She would live life to the full while she could, she said. She had six wonderful months with her beautiful baby and she loved every minute they spent together."

I couldn't equate this determined, self-sacrificing woman with the Jazz who'd pulled me into the Stationary Cupboard and had her wicked way with me. All the names I'd called her. The hatred I'd felt for her. Now this.

"And then a week ago, Jazz started to go downhill very fast. She told me that she wanted to give Misty to you. You're a good man, she told us. You'll take care of her. Mum and Dad begged her not to give her baby away to a stranger. But he's not a stranger, she insisted. He's the father of my child. He'll raise her, I know he will. They pleaded with her to let them keep Misty but she wasn't having any of it."

I swallowed the lump in my throat.

"And the rest you know. She arranged for Misty to be delivered to you at work. Then yesterday she died."

Both of us were crying now. I reached out for Poppy's hand.

"Why didn't she tell me this?" I asked, between sobs. "Why not tell me about Misty? I would have been there for her. For them both. Why the drama of having my baby delivered to me in a cardboard box at the office? Why the secrecy?"

"That was my sister all over," said Poppy sadly. "She had a wicked sense of humour. And anyway, she knew you'd work it out." She let go of my hand. "That's why I came round tonight. I wanted to check that you had Misty and that she was okay. And she is."

She stroked Silkie's cheek softly. The baby didn't stir.

"What about your family, Rob? And your friends? What do they think about you being a father?"

"My parents don't know. I haven't told them yet. The only people who know are from the office and Ahmed and his wife from the off-licence downstairs. My landlord. He's a good bloke."

"What do you think they'll say? Your parents?"

"It'll be a bit of shock for them. It's out of character for me, doing something like this. But they'll be fine with it. They're good people. Becca, that's my sister, she'll be wonderful about it too. They'll all help me raise Silkie. I know they will."

Poppy was quiet for a moment.

"I'd like to as well."

"As well as what?"

"I'd like to help raise her too. She's my niece. I'd like to be part of her life and help bring her up as well. And my parents."

I sat back. I should have seen that coming. But was this the 7th Cavalry I could hear coming over the hill? The answer to all my problems if I wanted it to be? Poppy and her parents, Silkie's grandparents, all wanting to look after my daughter. In my mind I saw a whole army not of horses but of Sheltand ponies galloping to my aid. It could be perfect. I could see my daughter when I wanted. Be part of her growing up but could get on with my life at the same time. This was a way out. And an easy one too. Guilt-free. And just for one moment, one very brief moment, I actually toyed with the idea.

༺───────༻

But how could I even think that? Jazz had clearly wanted me to have our baby after she died. There was no doubt in my mind now that Silkie was ours, Jazz's and mine, despite all the nonsense she'd told me about her questionable hobby. Somehow it felt right. And although there were much easier ways of telling me I was the father, and delivering her to me, Jazz had gone to great lengths to ensure I would have no option but to take her. How I wish though, I could have been part of Silkie's life right from the beginning, and part of Jazz's too, when I might have been able to help. But she'd obviously been supremely independent and I could empathise with that. She'd chosen not to have me in her life after our little interlude. Would she have thought differently if she hadn't been ill? I would never know. But, against her parents' wishes, there was absolutely no doubt she wanted me to have Silkie. Or should I call her Misty now?

"Penny for them," said Poppy, interrupting my thoughts.

It was dark now and she'd turned on the lights and closed the curtains. Silkie was lying on the rug trying to put her toes in her mouth.

"I was just wondering what I should call her. Now I know the name Jazz gave her."

"Whatever you decide, it'll be right."

Silkie rolled over onto her stomach, tucking her knees under her and sticking her bum up in the air.

"Wow! That's clever."

"I think she's going to be crawling before too long," said Poppy.

This was so exciting. My daughter. About to crawl. That had to be a Shetland pony moment. The first of many. We watched her in silence.

"Shouldn't I be putting her to bed?" I asked.

Poppy shook her head.

"She's alright as she is for the moment. I'd let her play."

She got up and went to make tea for us both. Making herself at home, I thought, worried.

"Will you be coming to the funeral?" she asked, handing me a mug.

"Of course I will," I told her emphatically. "And I'll be bringing Silkie."

"I'm glad. And my parents will be too. They'd want you there."

"Do they know you're here?"

Poppy nodded. "I told them I'd found out where you lived. That I was going to come and see you. Make sure everything was okay with you both."

"What did they say?"

"They want to meet you as soon as possible. They want to see their granddaughter too."

"They won't try and take her away from me will they?"

"I don't think so. You're her father. They recognise that. And a parent trumps a grandparent any day."

This, I realised, was my biggest fear. That someone would try and take my daughter away from me. Having just got her, the last thing I wanted was to lose her. How quickly things change. Three days ago I had my own solitary life with no-one to worry about but me. Suddenly that had been flipped on its head in a way I could never have imagined. This little bundle had entered my life and my whole world was different. Everything I did would have to change. There were two of us to care for now. And whilst I was terrified beyond belief I was hugely excited at the same time. I'd never been a father before. Would I know what to do? I couldn't ever remember having a feeling like this before, and d'you know what? I loved it. A thrill ran through my body as I watched my daughter pump her legs backwards and forwards. Crawling. Walking. Nursery. School. Each one a Shetland pony moment. And I would be part of it all. I had someone to share my life and I could not have been happier. Poppy saw the smile on my face.

"What?" she asked.

"Just planning," I told her.

"We've got a whole load of Misty's stuff at home. Clothes and toys and such. Can I bring them round tomorrow?"

"That would be good. But ring me first. I have to go into the office. I've only got two days' leave. I need to sort things out there."

"Like paternity leave?"

"Of course! I'm entitled to paternity leave, aren't I?"

I wondered what Ted would think about that!

Just saying the words out loud made me feel proud. Suddenly I was a man. A parent. And my life had taken on a whole new dimension. From small and insignificant, it was big and growing. And both Silkie and I would grow with it. We'd have our own Shetland pony moments together. Hundreds of them. And would our lives include Poppy? Yes, but only as Silkie's aunt and not in the way I rather suspected she thought it might. No, she could never replace Jazz, a selfless, loving woman, the mother of my child, who was special in a way no other person could be. Was it possible to fall in love with an image? With someone who was dead? I didn't know the answer to that but I certainly had feelings for Jazz I'd never felt for anyone before. Someone whom I'd never really known. A festive leg-over didn't count but there was more to it than that. The outcome of our brief liaison had had huge implications and changed the course of my life. Silkie would hear all about her and what a wonderful person she was. So now I had a future. We had a future. Me and my daughter.

"I'll leave you two to it," said Poppy, standing up. "See you tomorrow."

I heard voices at the door. Who was Poppy talking to?

Becca bounded up the stairs.

"I wasn't expecting you!" I cried. "What happened to Romania?"

"We finished filming early so I got the first flight home. What's that?" she demanded pointing at Silkie, who was happily rolling over and over.

"This is my daughter. That's what I wanted to tell you on the phone the other night. I'm a Dad!"

Becca looked at me in utter disbelief.

"You? A father? That's not possible! No way!"

"Way!" I told her smiling.

Was now the time to tell her about the Christmas party and Jazz? She'd understand. So, finally, I told my sister everything that had happened. By the time I'd finished, Silkie, exhausted with all her strenuous attempts to crawl, was in the mood for food.

"Can I hold her?" asked Becca.

She picked Silkie up off the floor as I went into the kitchen to make up her formula.

"Isn't she gorgeous? Hard to believe, isn't it, that I'm her dad?"

"How sure are you that you are the father?"

I gave Becca the bottle, not liking her question.

"What do you mean? Why are you asking me that? I told you that Poppy said Jazz bragged about how many people she slept with. And that most of them would have been women. Look at her hair, though. It's the spit of mine."

Silkie sucked at the bottle noisily.

"And I feel that she's mine. She just is."

"It's been what? Two days?" asked Becca. "How can you feel that she's yours in that short time?"

"I don't know. But I can."

Why was my sister doing this?

"I hate to spoil everything, Rob, but she can't possibly be yours."

"Why not?" My mouth was dry.

"Somebody's having you on."

"What? What are you talking about?"

"Have you got anything to drink in this place?"

I shook my head. "Nothing here but there's an off-licence downstairs."

Becca was gone five minutes and returned with a wine box. I raised my eyebrows.

"Heavy night?" I asked her.

"It may just be," she replied as she found a large wine glass in one of the kitchen cabinets and filled it to the brim. "You might want to put Silkie to bed. I don't think she should hear this."

"She's only a baby!" I laughed. "Anyway," I was more serious now, "what is it she shouldn't hear?"

Becca drained half the glass.

"Remember when you were young? You had to go into hospital?"

"Yeh. I was about 6 or 7, something like that."

"You had some sort of infection. Some long name they called it. It messed up your hormones and you were quite ill at the time. Anyway, the doctors said it could affect you in later life"

"Affect me? How?"

"Did Mum and Dad never tell you this?"

"I think I'd have remembered."

"I can't believe it's me having to tell you." She took another drink. "Well, apparently, they were told that it could affect your fertility. Your ability to have children."

"Could?" I asked her.

"More than could."

I took a gulp from Becca's glass and mulled over what she'd just said. If what she said was true, then the one, single, unalterable fact was that in all likelihood, I was not Silkie's father. And if I wasn't, who was? Becca had just shattered my entire world. I had no claim to this baby. She wasn't mine. Without another word I took my daughter from my sister and went up to bed.

Sorry? Not for one minute!

Silkie starts junior school tomorrow and we've both decided it's a three Shetland pony day. She's marked it off on a special calendar her aunt Poppy bought her – each month has a different picture of a pony – and she's attached three stickers of ponies that her other aunt, Becca, bought her, on the very important date, September 7th. Silkie has had many smaller days – her first tooth, toddling, birthdays, Christmases, her last ever nappy day, primary school – there's been lots of them but both of us thought that tomorrow was worthy of a full three Shetland pony accolade. She's already tried her new uniform on more times than I can count and I've taken lots of photos for both sets of grandparents. How grown-up she looks.

Obviously I'd decided to keep her. Becca had tried to persuade me otherwise but deep down, right from the start, Silkie always felt like she was my daughter. And it didn't matter if she wasn't. Jazz had wanted me to have her and that was good enough for me. Poppy and her parents, Silkie's grandparents, unaware of my medical issues, as indeed was I for a very long time, firmly believe she was mine. And if my parents had any reservations, they've never said a word to me. They love their granddaughter unconditionally. And Becca? She adores her niece as I knew she would.

I can't pretend it's been easy, balancing work and a growing child, but everyone has rallied round, including Ahmed and Ayesha, who do everything in their power to spoil Silkie something rotten. Yes, I've kept her name. Perhaps it wasn't the most inspired choice initially but I've grown to like it.

And me? I'm still in the same job, and promoted now. I took over from Ted when he decided he'd had enough but I choose not to occupy the Stationary Cupboard! I had to rent a bigger place when Silkie outgrew her drawer. Once again, Ahmed helped me out there. And now every day for me now is a three Shetland pony day. My life is big. Full. I'm still young, only just turned 26, so it's almost like Silkie and I are growing up together. What's not to like?

Hands, Knees and...

My cabin at midnight, he whispered in her ear.

She set her alarm, just in case.

1155. Time to go.

She tried to stand. Nothing. Her knees had locked in arthritic defiance.

Unable to move, she lay on her bed, sobbing, imagining

the handsome stranger making love to someone whose knees bent beautifully.

ACKNOWLEDGEMENTS

Once again a huge thank you to my back-up team; Piers, the IT wizard and cover designer, and my proof-reading team, Glyn, Chris, Angela and Lynn.

Where am I going to put all those spare apostrophes?

Don't answer that!

And a very big thank you to you for reading my book. I really hope you enjoyed it. I would be grateful if you could review it on Amazon for me
– I read every review and they all help shape my future work.

Thankyou.

— Maggie Whitley

Maggie Whitley lives in Yorkshire.
This is her tenth book.

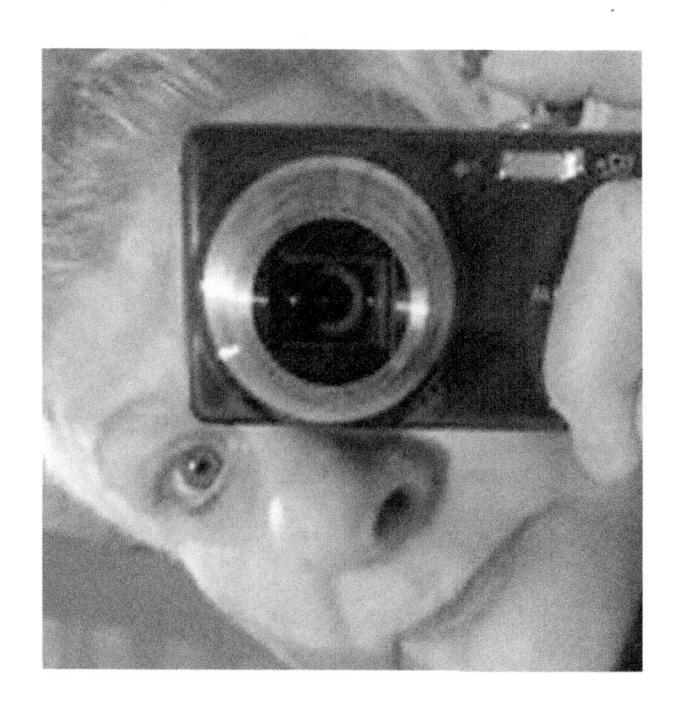